THE LAST MARK

THE LAST MARK

D.T. SMITH

Copyright © 2021 by D.T. Smith

All rights reserved. No part of this book may be reproduced in any form or by any electronic or mechanical means including information storage and retrieval systems without permission in writing from the publisher, except by a reviewer, who may quote brief passages in a review.

Published in the United States by D.T. Smith

First Edition

This is a work of fiction. Names, characters, places and events either are the product of the author's imagination or are used fictitiously. Any similarity to real persons, living or dead, is coincidental and not intended by the author.

ISBN 978-8-7708-6898-2

Edited by Matthew Dowd

CHAPTER 1

The sound of chains encountering other chains fills the dead room. The light, slowly pouring through the cracks of the old, and what seems to be, dry rotted boards making up the walls of this place. Struggling to gather myself, breathing shallowly. It is as if someone is pulling the threads of my consciousness and preventing what I so desperately wanted to be, awake. Suddenly, I hear a door being opened, like someone had pulled back on a large metal latch. Shaking and breathing a little more heavily at this point, I could not help but notice the smell coming from this place. It smelled of old dust, copper, almost like if you had a penny in your mouth and could smell a taste. Just as I was finishing my thought, I saw a figure coming from around the corner. A tall and dark figure billowing over what a normal sized human could naturally be. Where the Hell am I?

***

"Detective!" Screeched the Chief of the Danville Police Department. "Yeah, Chief?" I replied, in an easy-going kind of tone. "Hodge, I told you 4 p.m. sharp! Now where have you been?!" He barked. I had still been trying to settle into my place since taking the job, and while finishing unpacking today, I had lost track of time. Hence, why the Chief had given me most of the day to finish up.

"Sir, I apologize. I must have lost track of time." The Chief turned and started walking back towards his office, still with a hint of anger in his body language. I followed closely behind and had been analyzing the situation since, I originally heard the chief raising his voice. Right before I could start talking, after carefully thinking of how to defuse the situation, Chief sat down and started staring at me, like he had just seen a ghost.

"Detective, I'm going to debrief you on a case I'd like to put you on. We have had fourteen young men go missing within the last four months over a twenty-mile radius." Chief as he was giving the debriefing had an overwhelming since of heaviness come over his chest. "The young boys are ages from eight to ten years old, and we anticipate the perp to strike again within 72 hours." Chief had barely gotten these words out of his mouth. It is not that Chief Smith has never seen bad cases before, or even ones as serious. But, when fourteen young men go missing in Kentucky, you tend to start feeling worried. In fact, when fourteen young men go missing anywhere in a short period of time, people start getting a little uneasy.

"Alright, Chief, what leads have we gotten so far?" I asked lightly. "Well, we have narrowed down the facts by picking up on the same abduction scenario. It appears these young boys are taken in the night from their homes." Chief said, embarrassed. I began to think how sorry it was that a Chief of Police could be so dense. "But the families have given us some photos of the boys to identify them."

"This criminal has been able to not only take these young boys without any detection but do it multiple times with no error." When you think of young boys, you start to imagine them trying to put up a fight to make a scene. But this situation didn't make much sense; the criminal was able to come in undetected, and not only take a young boy against their will but do it without any sign of struggle in a home where their parents are most likely right down the hall!

I had been running all these bits of information through my head since the Chief had started briefing, but there is one thing that stuck out to me. "Chief, has there been any recoveries of the boys since all this started?" I asked with little hope.

"I'm afraid not son, but the families like I said, have given us some photos of the boys to identify them." Chief picked up the stack of photos enclosed in the case file and passed them over the desk towards me. "Is there anything that sticks out to you, maybe even that can give you an idea of a motive?"

I picked up the case file, and when I opened the file and went through some of the photos. My eyes widened, and a sudden heaviness burdened my chest. Sweat beginning to bead up on my brow, even though it was perfectly cool inside the office. Much like the Chief had wondered, I immediately started having a sense of déjà vu. This feeling is not something that happens often to myself, so how to respond to it is difficult for me.

"Hodge? What is with you? You look like something is on your mind? Did something stick out to you?"

"It's nothing. I'm going to go and check the system really quick. See if any other cases like this have been going on in counties around us. Maybe this is all connected to some kind of child trafficking." As soon as I had the Chief's facial expression shifted.

"Sure, go ahead, and see what you can find."

I made my way out into the station and sat down at my desk. I couldn't help but notice all the other officers looking at me in almost shifts. A few would turn to me, then another few. Almost as if they were trying to see what I was doing. I turned to my computer and started to ignore it. It was all just probably in my head, being new and having the anxiety of not knowing anyone.

I attempted to log into my computer but kept giving an error message. Trying multiple times to see if had just left some characters out of the password given to me, but nothing was working.

"Hey, Chief! Have my log-in credentials you gave me changed?" The Chief came to the doorway of his office and gave me a frustrated look.

"These computers! Always having issues! I'll have to get one of the technical people to look at it. I'm sorry, Detective, it might be a while before you can get in."

"Well, that's alright, Chief, do you mind me using someone else's computer to look at this information?"

"Detective, you should know by now that's against security regulations. I can't allow you to do that, but why don't you go ahead and ask one of the other officers here to get the information you need?"

I turned to look at the officer closest to me and asked, "Would you be able to search the surrounding counties to see if they have any missing child cases? I'm wanting to see if this could be linked to something bigger, such as a trafficking case."

The officer looked at me and said nothing but answered with a simple nod. He started looking down at his computer and began to type.

I waited patiently as he was searching the database for the answers I was wanting. But after some time had passed, he finally turned to me.

"I couldn't find any cases of missing children in the surrounding counties for the past few decades. I'm sorry, seems like you are just as stumped as we are about the whole situation."

"I appreciate the help, can I let you know if I need anything else from the database while my credentials are being taken care of?" The officer turned to me and again answered with just a simple nod. So, I got up and went back over to the Chief's office and poked my head in.

"Chief, do you mind if I take this file with me? I would like to go over it some tonight." In the back of my mind, something was clawing, trying to get out. This feeling was causing anxiety and nausea; something is not right.

"No, I don't care if you take it with you, but try and get some sleep." Knowing good and well that I would take this file and be examining all aspects of it through the night. I started walking back through the station, hearing whispering from the other officers as I was passing made me feel a little unsettled. It was as if the whole department had just been examining me, but not in the way to make sure I was doing my job. No, it seemed more along the lines of they already knew of me and couldn't believe I was here.

I've always had a bit of a hard time making friends or even getting close to anyone, but this seemed different. Like, they all knew something I didn't; like, I was stepping into something terrible or maybe hopeless.

CHAPTER 2

I made my way down to my vehicle and started to head home. Passing streetlights and seeing the fast glare of orange hit across the hood of the vehicle. Thoughts flaring up like confusion and anger for not understanding, or maybe remembering.

What is this? The memory so close, yet so far from grasp? What has happened to me where I would suppress a memory? It is probably nothing, just all in my mind. I have probably just seen or read some recent story that reminded me of this. It is just in my head, lack of sleep, and the lack of food probably triggered an emotional response, simple. It must be, there is no other explanation that would make any sense.

***

I pulled up to the house I had recently bought. A three bedroom and two-bathroom ranch style house. I never had much of a family, but I've always felt like one day I might be able to. I had an internal want for family since I was a young child. Being raised in foster care all through my young life, I began to fantasize about what a life will be like when I'm older and have a family of my own. To come in every day to someone you call a "significant" other. One who shares a bond so strong it's significant in description, as well as irreplaceable. I thought of having a few children, someone that could always be excited to see me, or someone that looks for me and points me out when being picked up from school. I didn't have that experience growing up, but I saw it through other kids that were around me. I never knew my parents, I was taken to a local foster home and left as an infant in Terre Haute, Indiana. I never had any more information about them, could have been why I got into law enforcement in the hopes of finding out why one day. But as I got older, I started to not want to know and realized I got along just fine on my own.

I struggled to pass the police academy due to my asthma, but somehow, I still managed. After passing I started working for the Terre Haut Police Department for a few years. The whole time while being on duty, I never had to draw my gun once. Most of the time, I never kept the mag in the gun. I've hated guns my whole life and have never really understood why. But I knew if I wanted to become a cop, I would have to learn to shoot and operate one. So, while in the academy, I was trained and became an excellent marksman. It never changed the fact I hated the weapon. Most of the time I just left the mag in the glove box of the squad car. Somehow, even with all my quirks I made it through. It wasn't long after I got an offer online to go down to Danville, Kentucky to take the position of detective. I couldn't pass up an offer to take the next step in my career; so, two weeks went by, and I had moved to my new home. It's been one week since then, and I feel I've settled in alright.

I got out of the car, and as soon as I did my face was greeted by a brisk rush of breeze. The kind that makes you squint from the sharp dagger-like winter air. I didn't have a garage at the moment, as it was taken up by the extra clutter I seemed to keep around over the years. I grabbed the file and my things, just trying to hurry up and get inside. Opening the door to the house I still got that feeling of new belonging, like the turning of a crisp new page to a book you started.

I dropped the file on to the desk in the study and began making way for the kitchen. I got out a glass, two ice cubes, and began pouring Jameson into the glass. Drank the first glass with one explosion of movement, as if taking a shot at a bachelor party for one of your best friends. I poured another, and at that point, grabbed the bottle and started heading back to the study.

As soon as I started to open the file, a large rumble shook the house; it was thunder from a storm that had begun pouring down rain. "Of course, it's storming!" I rolled my eyes and began to try and regain focus to this case, starting to read where I left off from the Chief's office. It appears the children had just turned ten years old. Fourteen young boys, being taken over the last few years, six within the last year. I started realizing more and more that the amount of time in between abductions has gotten smaller and smaller. The last boy's name was Charlie Mitchell, nine years old, and lived right outside Parksville, Kentucky. Taken about two months ago, and forensics found absolutely nothing in the home. Charlie was taken in the night and no prints left from the abductor at the house. So, the abductor is good, and starting to get more confident.

According to the time in between the last two abductions, the abductor would strike again within the next few days. I started pulling out the photos from the file again and stuck to the back of one of the photos I viewed earlier was another photo. It appears this one was of the last child abducted as well, Charlie Mitchell. My eyes were stuck on the picture, focused, and could not be drawn away from it. There was a mark on the victim. It was on his arm, on his left side, barely visible as the mark was all white. Looking to be two triangles over lapping, with points rising from both sides of the top one, and a flipped cross emerging from the bottom. A mark that would probably bring questions, and torment growing up. A mark that would always influence self-questioning, a mark that was identical to mine.

CHAPTER 3

A loud obnoxious noise had woken me up, kind of like an extreme hazmat alarm at a chemical plant. But it was just my alarm on I had set on my phone. Six-thirty a.m. had come so fast, and it never ceased to amaze me how fast I could lose time I needed. I stood up from my desk, which I had fallen asleep working at once again. My neck just barely able to turn thanks to sleeping wrong and causing a crick in it. While walking down the hall, I slowly tried easing my neck the opposite way to remedy the discomfort. As I figured, it did nothing for the discomfort but make it somewhat more uncomfortable.

    I reached the bathroom to start my routine. Since I was around ten years old, it has helped me to keep a set schedule for myself to feel a bit more in control. Shower at 6:30, brushing teeth and combing hair at 6:45, and getting dressed at 6:55. After this first step in my routine, I usually made breakfast. But this morning I had to get down to the station and speak to Chief Smith about my findings. I could not get that mark out of my head.

***

While pulling up to the station, I noticed an unusual number of cars parked outside. This had me start with all the *what ifs*. But that could not get in my way right now, they're too many lives at stake. I started to get out of the car and head towards the doors. Even though the circumstances are unknown, the anticipation has made my chest feel like a cage holding a savage animal trying to escape.

I opened the door to the station and began heading towards the Chief's office. I can't help but to overhear a conversation between an officer and a husband and wife. It appears that couple is here because their little boy had been abducted from their home sometime in the night. It appears their name is the Petersons, and their boy is Aiden; the other people were concerned citizens from town. Our predictions were off, the abductor had already taken another child.

I see Chief Smith and make a notion to speak with him. Chief makes a motion with his arm in return, looking as if he was making a meaningless attempt to fan himself, even though it was to say, "Come on." The sound of the Chiefs office door closing was very subtle, as he was trying to not attract any extra attention.

"Travis, another child has been abducted in the night." said Chief Smith with stress entangled within his statement. "I know, Aiden Peterson."

"How did you already know that?"

"I was listening to the details of the conversation as I was walking in. But, Chief, how did all the other people here find out?" The Chief started looking towards the Petersons with such irritation and disgust.

"Well, you can thank the Petersons for that, apparently they don't have much faith in the police, even in desperate moments. So, they informed everyone they could get ahold of to get his image and name out there. Now, we have multiple towns people worried and being frantic." I started analyzing the situation, thinking if the town had started being in a state of hysteria it would give the abductor a better opportunity to find more children. What was his game! Assuming it was a male abducting the children. Was it sex trafficking? Could it be for child slavery? Is the abductor taking the children and having their way with them, and afterwards killing them?

CRACK! The door slams back up against the wall as one of the officers from the front desk barges through it. "Chief, a mother is out here screaming her child has been taken," said the officer.

"I know, we have been dealing with Mrs. Peterson all morning," said Chief Smith.

"No, Chief, this one just came in and is very frantic sir!" the officer responded. Chief immediately started walking out to the front corridor to meet the woman, he could hear her screaming from here.

"You! Are you in charge here! You are supposed to be finding all these children! Protecting the city!" the scared mother belted. "Are you some kind of detective!" said the mother, looking at me with such frustration and little hope. I knew something needed to be said other than the normal, *'we are doing all we can.'* I looked her in the eyes and said, "Ma'am, I cannot imagine what you are going through.

Honestly, I cannot imagine being as strong as you are being about it. But I've just taken over this case and I will do whatever it takes to find your son and the other boys."

The woman looked at me and started to cry, but you could see her guard has lowered just enough that we may be able to ask some questions to help identify the boy. I took her to a room away from the crowd of reporters and the Petersons. We sat down and I asked her, "Can I get you some coffee, or hot tea?" Instead of answering with her words, the woman could only bring herself to nod. I handed the woman the hot drink and some tissues.

"Alright, ma'am, what's your son's name?" The woman looked up and said, "His name is Austin, Austin Douglas." I was writing the information down as I heard it. "What is your name miss and where was your child last seen?"

"My name is Kelly Douglas; he was put to bed around eight-thirty last night in our home. Our address is 766 Mercury Crest Drive, right outside Danville." I stopped while writing and looked up at Kelly and said, "I know this has to be hard for you, but any details can be critical at this point."

"Detective, it's just me and my son. His father left us after he was born; he's all I have," Kelly said with desperation. "Kelly, do you have any photos of Austin that I can use to help us identify him?" Kelly started digging through her bag. Hands shaking from the anxiety, she was able to find her wallet, and put it on the table.

"I have one in my wallet, it's not really a great picture. It was taken this last summer while he was playing outside in the sprinkler." I took the picture and froze. Staring at the photo with such intent Kelly began to question the quality of the photo for the investigation. "Detective, will that work?" Still stuck looking at the photo, head racing with so many questions.

"Kelly, this mark on Austin, how long has that been there?" Kelly leaned into the photo and looked at what I had pointed out.

"Oh that? That is just a birthmark, it's been there since he was born."

My mind is spinning. This cannot be, how could Austin have the same birth mark as not only Charlie Mitchell, a previous child that had been abducted, but me as well. A shiver ran down my spine, causing me to jerk a little bit.

"Thank you for all the information, I'm going to start going over this and will head out to your house here shortly." Kelly stood up and thanked me, but her body language has changed. As if she just got finished with a job interview, and the results were better than expected. Almost like she was… relieved.

CHAPTER 4

I had broken out into a cold sweat, as I dwelled on the experience that I just had with that woman. It was as if I had the flu, having a high temperature, but still freezing cold. She was so distressed when she came in. Why would she be relieved when leaving? Was it a kind of comfort given by talking to me, a detective? No, it could not be anything like that, especially after she treated the Chief in such a way prior to speaking to me. Was it an act?

I head towards the Chief's office to let him know I am headed over to the Douglas place. I did not realize I had been sitting in the meeting room for over an hour after speaking with Ms. Douglas.

"Chief, I'm heading over to the Douglas's house." I said, with hesitation in my voice. "Well, Travis, the Forensics should already be there. Call me with any updates. I need to stay here and try to keep things at bay."

I started heading for my car, and the whole time I kept thinking of the birth marks found on the children and myself. I also couldn't stop thinking about the change in body language that Ms. Douglas had after speaking with me. This whole situation is not adding up.

The drive over 766 Mercury Crest Drive seemed to be longer than the amount of time that Google Maps had portrayed. This phenomenon could be because I couldn't stop thinking of a way that the birth marks tie into all of this, and if they did, how he ended up with the same one. Years before these children went missing, I was born with the same birth mark. The odds of this happening are so low, that it would be foolish to not think it is connecting us all somehow.

I pulled up to the home and saw the forensic team coming in and out, gathering data. Walking up to the house I stopped one of the team members and asked "Have we found any sign of the abductor? Any sign of struggle?"

"No sir, we haven't found any evidence of a break in, or any struggle from the abduction. Honestly, we haven't found any signs of disturbance what-so-ever," said the young forensic specialist. The team member could see the troubled and quite puzzled look on my face, I am sure. "Sir, do we have any ideas or clues on to who is doing this yet?" I looked at him with such a face it made the team member question any hope that could be had in this.

"I'm going to go take a look around the house." I told him with a double intention, one to get me away from the conversation that I had nothing to contribute to, and two, I have hope that the house will reveal some missing pieces.

I made my way to the house and through the door, only to notice the team was packing up and leaving. It appears that Ms. Douglas was not in the house, possibly to speak with the team outside, or maybe even working on getting neighbors to help look. All I know is that this is an opportunity to investigate Ms. Douglas and her past. The way she changed after speaking with me is still stuck on my mind.

Digging through papers, and photo albums, nothing is showing any signs of wrongdoing. I started heading towards the mother's room, and on my way up the stairs my heart started pounding at a rate at which I thought it would jump out of my chest. My palms began sweating, and head pounding. Reaching the upstairs, I turned and saw the open door to Austin's room. Turning the other way to look, I could see another few rooms with closed doors down the hall. "I had not realized this house was so big. It is definitely deceptive from the outside."

I made my way over to Austin's room and started looking around. There were Lego bricks on what seemed to be a designated table for building. There were also some kind of monster cartoon characters on posters on the wall. The glow in the dark planets stuck on the ceiling were noticeable as well. Tonka and RC crafts organized in the corner of the room. And to top of the décor of the child's room, there was a Pokémon lamp beside the bed. But, besides the décor, I started seeing other details. Windows look like they have never been open and room so clean. This does not make any sense, how could there be no sign of struggle, no sign of anyone being in here. The abductor has perfected his craft for sure, especially with a parent in the home. But, how far down the hall exactly is Ms. Douglas's room?

Walking down the hall I open the next door on the left, it's just a guest bathroom. Walking further opening the second door, it was a storage closet which apparently is kept stocked with cleaning supplies. Walking further down the hall the next door I stop in front of and begins to open it. It has a subtle creak as it opens. Like you would hear in a movie when someone was opening the door to the last house they would ever see. As eerie as the door sounded, the bedroom looked as plain as a room could have. Wallpaper covering all sections of the wall, with a simple floral print. Looking to be a honeysuckle pattern, running down from the ceiling to the floor. The bed frame was an old white metal frame, square style, with a queen size mattress and plain white sheets and comforter. Unlike Austin's room, there was not any sign of personalization, no décor, no home feeling. It is as if the woman thought of the bedroom only as a function, not a personal space.

I started going towards the dresser, opening drawers only to reveal clothes with nothing hidden underneath them. While walking over to the other side of the room, I felt a small draft. Looking back at the windows to ensure they were shut, I started looking towards the wall that I was walking adjacent with. Quickly looking down at the floor I immediately saw lite scraping, where it appears a section of the wall had been moved to make a door. I started running my fingertips along the section of the wall, feeling a very small gap where the paper can be pressed in. I placed my palm on it and firmly pressed, and when I did a I heard a "click" of release. It appeared to a magnetize strip keeping the section of the wall in contact, like a mirrored medicine cabinet. I fully pulled the section of wall back to reveal a door.

The door was faded in color, but originally appearing to be a darker brown. Instead of a traditional doorknob, it was a heavy latch bar, and a handle to pull shut. Slowly reaching towards the handle, hands shaking, I grasped both the latch and the handle and pushed. A small gust had come out towards my face, as if you were opening a sealed door on an airplane to exit. It was dark on the staircase pass this door, lurking like the kind of darkness you would see with an abandoned house.

"Wait, we are on the second level of the house? Is the staircase running in between one of the walls dividing the rooms downstairs?" I questioned aloud to myself. I started feeling for a light switch, hands running across the wall searching, when I felt a small shelf that seemed to have a flashlight on it. Picking up the flashlight and turning it on, I began proceeding into wherever this is taking me. Counting the stairs as I take them, I cannot believe the amount that has already been taken, and yet no bottom. But then I see it, the bottom. Flashing the light towards the wall before turning, seeing a switch. I flip it on, only to reveal a nice set of table and chairs, and a light piece above it that anyone would be proud to call theirs. What kind of person has these kinds of things hidden below the house?

Walking to the other side of the room lies what appears to be a large book cradled by a tripod rack for it. It had a symbol on the cover, one triangle upside down, another lapping over it right side up. It looked like antlers out of the top, and on the bottom of the triangle a upside down cross maybe. Apparently, it has significant value to it. If it didn't why would it appear to be in the middle of the room? Getting closer to opening the book, hands sweating, and heart pounding, I began to open it. "What the Hell?" It was a photo album of the Douglas family. Flipping through pages, seeing birthday parties, holidays, and even losing Austin's first tooth. Why would this be down here? Why is a family album hidden in an offset basement? Then suddenly, I hear footsteps next to me, on the other side of the wall. I must be on the opposite side of the stairs leading to the second level, and it sounds as if the steps were going up the stairs.

CHAPTER 5

As the steps seemed to be coming closer to Mrs. Douglas's room, I started towards the stairs to get out of this weird, off set living room. Running up the staircase as light footed as possible, reaching the top and closing the door behind me. The footsteps coming down the hall were drawing near, so I started moving the bookshelf back in front of the door. As soon as I turn around Mrs. Douglas walks in the room, and stares with wide eyes without saying a word.

I was not sure how to start this off, but luckily Mrs. Douglas did for me. "Detective? I thought everyone had left and had gotten all the information they could?" she said with curiosity, and fear in her voice.

"Well, Mrs. Douglas, I had come later and was trying to uncover any information that might give us a lead to how the abductor had gotten into your home undetected." I did not want her knowing I was uncovering things about this small family of theirs. Whatever that hidden basement was about, I knew she did not want me knowing about it.

"Well, Detective Hodge, I'd like to get some sleep now if you don't mind. I can't get rid of this headache and want to try and sleep it off."

"Of course, this stress has to be overwhelming for you. I cannot imagine going through what you are. It is taking a toll on you, I'm sure."

I started towards the staircase, but as I drew nearer to the bedroom door, I noticed that Mrs. Douglas was not moving to make an opening. "Excuse me, ma'am." Once I had said something, it is like she did not even think to move, like her mind was racing in a thousand different directions. I started down the staircase and to the front door, but as I looked back to say goodbye, I immediately got a chilling sensation over my body. Seeing her standing at the top of the stairs, looking down at me so quietly and empty.

"Have a good afternoon, Mrs. Douglas, get some rest." After saying that she stared at me for a moment, then after thirty or forty seconds she slowly raised her right hand to wave me on. That chill deepened within my body, like seeing an eerie image that just cannot escape your mind. This woman has something off about her; after everything, I still cannot seem to figure it out.

As I was leaving the Douglas place, my phone started to ring. I never really cared too much for putting an actual song for my ringtone, but rather just a classic telephone ring. Anyway, I did not feel like speaking on the phone now, so I let it go to voicemail.

Why did they have a living room setting hidden? What exactly was so significant about the photo album that was held on a pedestal? Maybe that was Mrs. Douglas's get away. A secret place she can go and feel comfortable, like a

"Man-Cave." Is the photo album just something that makes her happy?

My mind was racing in so many directions with questions, nothing is adding up. But one thing is for certain, Mrs. Douglas has not been truthful. She has been hiding something since the start of all of this, I am just not sure how or why.

Just as I was pulling into the station, my cell starts to ring. Chief Smith is what the I.D. on the phone read. I answered the phone by saying, "What's up, Chief?"

"Travis, where the Hell have you been? I've been calling and left a voicemail! It's past noon and I can't get ahold of you!"

"Sorry, Chief, I was back out at the Douglas's place. I was trying to see if there was anything Forensics might have missed from earlier."

"Be that as it may, Hodge, I need to be able to get ahold you with this kind of case going! We've had more parents come in, and we are up to eighteen children missing!"

"How can this be? How can so many children go missing at once? Are we dealing with a team here, a group for trafficking? How is this even possible?" I couldn't make any sense of this; nothing was adding up. All I could figure out so far was something was off with Mrs. Douglas, and she knows more than she is letting on. I also know that these children, having the same identical birth mark as I had couldn't be a coincidence.

Something was terribly wrong, and I'm not sure how to even approach it. But, if all of this had been going on and cases of children kept piling up why wasn't there any help from the feds. I'm afraid I've stepped into a much bigger case than anticipated.

CHAPTER 6

Walking up to the station, I could hear the commotion inside through the door. Parents crying, the sound of sobbing echoing throughout the building.

"Hodge!" screamed out the Chief from across the room."

I walked into his office, and he shut the door behind me. I could see from his facial expression and body language he was passed overwhelmed.

"What is going on, Chief! I can't imagine that ALL of these people's children just were abducted in one night!"

"If I knew what the Hell was going on don't you think we would be in a complete different situation? We have all the photos and files built for these children missing, look at these and see if you make any connection, Hodge."

I took the files from him and started to go through the first few. It was starting to be apparent what was becoming the trend between these cases. Every abduction happened during the night, with no sign of break-in.

"Chief, how is it that someone can be breaking into these homes without their parents noticing as well as without leaving any evidence of that fact afterwards?"

Suddenly, Chief Smith stands up as one of the officers in the front is signaling for him with a sense of urgency. Chief waves him on to come in the office.

"Chief, there is a man claiming that he witnessed something last night. He lives on the same street as the Douglas family."

"A witness! Bring him into the conference room so we can get a statement!" Chief said with such gusto.

"Hodge, I need you to go and collect this statement. I need you to pay very close attention to detail on this and see if we can get some kind of lead."

"Alright, Chief." I was having a lot of doubt that this witness would be worth something, but anything at this point is better than nothing.

I started walking towards the conference room, and on my way, I see the man starting to sit down in there. It was a middle-aged man with darker hair combed to the side and older looking glasses. He wore a blue and white plaid button-up shirt, and light-colored blue jeans. I walked in and introduced myself to the man.

"Hello, I'm Detective Travis Hodge and I'm the head on this investigation. The officer out there said you might have some information on one of the abductions that could help?"

"I believe I do; my name is Gerard Glover. I live just right down the block from the Douglas family. But I'm not sure you will believe me and what I have to say," he said with such hesitation.

"I will listen to whatever it is you saw or even think you saw. Nothing is too little in this kind of case. So, why don't you start from the beginning and tell me step by step what happened and how you saw it."

"Well, I was outside pretty late taking my dog on a walk because it is good for his joints. When I got down to the Douglas family's house, I saw something in their front yard staring up at one of the windows on the house. When I…"

"Wait, what do you mean 'something?' Do you mean you saw someone looking up at the house?"

"Sir, I said, 'something,' because I am not one hundred percent on what it could have been. It was a very large and a dark shadow figure standing in front of the house. It looked to be about eight feet tall. The person, or thing was standing there as if they were waiting on something. So, I took my dog down the sidewalk farther trying to put distance in between myself and the figure. As I was getting farther away, I saw the being move for the first time and made its way into the house by the front door."

"Alright sir, you are telling me this person took the front door to go inside this home?"

"Yes, Detective, it stood there and all of sudden it went through the front door like someone had to let him in. I swear. That's why after I heard that these kids had gotten abducted, I came in immediately. Thought maybe it could help somehow in figuring out who did it."

"Did this person see you at all since you were on the other side of the street? It seems unlikely that they would not have seen someone if they were doing something like this. Wouldn't you watch your back and your surroundings if you were going to do something like this?"

"I understand how it must sound, but it just ended up happening this way. I cannot say one way or the other why it did not see me. I just know that it had not seen me when I was nearby. If it did, I did not notice it looking in my direction."

"Well, sir, I really appreciate this information. If we need you for anything else, I will give you call."

"Detective, I know it sounds unreal. Truly, I know it sounds like I fabricated this story. But I cared about Austin Douglas. That child since he was a boy would come over on his weekends and help me in the yard or whatever I was doing if he saw I was out. Never wanted anything as payment, just simply wanting to help. So, anything I can do to help bring him back to safety I will."

I sat there trying to process this all for a moment. The fact that if this man was telling the truth and not looking for a couple minutes of fame, whoever is taking these children was able to just walk in using the front door. If this was so, did someone open the door for this person?

CHAPTER 7

As I was watching Mr. Glover walk out of the station, Chief started in my direction. I'm guessing he is wanting to go over what information we might have gotten from the witness. But the look on his face is saying something completely different.

"Hodge, did the witness's testimony hold any value? We could really use a win right now."

"Chief, I'm not sure we would want this kind of testimony getting out to the all the people in town. It sounds like this man does his fair share of drinking and might have mistaken what really happened. He claimed he saw a dark shadowed figure standing in front of the Douglas home, like it was waiting for something."

"Oh, well, regardless of what the old man said, you have other testimonies to go through from the parents that came in while you were at the Douglas house. Up until now you just have read the complete case files that we had from the past months."

"Alright, I'm going to take them with me and go grab some food. I'm going to grab a burger; do you want anything chief?"

"Of course, I do, Hodge, but you know my wife has me on this crappy healthy diet. Saying at my age, 'I need to watch my cholesterol.'"

I could see how he was upset about the diet, but at the same time didn't really care at the moment. Since this situation started, it seems like the Chief has been getting more and more grief from the community. Being the Chief of Police while something like this is going on can really dampen the image you have with the community you are supposed to be keeping safe from harm.

I started gathering up all the files and paperwork, wrapped the stack with an oversized rubber band. I have always found pleasure in the sound that a rubber band makes when it is stretched thin, and accidentally hit it like a strum to a base guitar. Nothing huge, and the sound does not last longer than a second or two, but something about it has always put a smile on my face.

I picked up the stack, that is now wrapped with the rubber band, and started for my car. Lunch is always so simple, if it wasn't eating Mexican style food, I was getting a burger from Sonic. One of the only places I can always count on for a solid burger, as well not forced into eating fries. I have never really enjoyed fries a lot. So, the tots I can get with the meal instead have always made me happy.

As I was driving, I kept going over the question that if Mr. Glover's testimony was true, did someone let this person, or being, in the house? Would it have been the parent? It could possibly be the child that let them in. Maybe they met this abductor online and grew to trust them. Whatever the case may be, it does explain how no sign of the abduction happening has been found so far. No struggle, or even forced entry. But am I ready to accept that some shadowy figure was lurking outside this home? That some fictional sized being was waiting the opportunity to be invited in, and abduct a child?

I got to the Sonic menu and leaned out of the window to push that iconic red button. I order the number one combo with tots and a Cherry Coke. After doing so, I pulled the stack of files over into my lap and started undoing the rubber band. Started to go through the files one by one. All the same exact story, it was in the night. Parents right down the hall and had no idea their child was being taken. No sign of entry, no sign of anything. I started looking through the photos provided, that is when I saw something that immediately made my stomach drop. In the background of one of the photos, where the family is standing in what appears to be a library, was the symbol I saw at the Douglas house on the photo album. It's on some type of plaque on the wall over the fireplace. My stomach is in knots, and I can barely think of eating now. But as soon as I complete my thought a CLACK, CLACK, CLACK hit beside me on the window. It was the roller skate waitress knocking on my window with a hand covered in rings. I rolled down the window and paid her for the food. But I could barely think of anything else at the moment. The same symbol that was found in Ms. Douglas's hidden offset living room was found in another family's photo.

I took the file that this photo came from, started going through it to read more about this family. Tim and Stephanie Morgan and their son, Chris, live on 814 Livingston Rd. Twenty-eight miles from the Douglas home, and in a much nicer part of the city. Whatever this symbol is or means, I think when I can figure it out; I'll be able to piece together an important link between these cases. I put in the address into my GPS and start heading over to the Morgan home.

The feeling you used to get as a child when the lights went out on you, and you were alone started taking over my stomach. The more I thought about what this all could mean, the more I started to conclude that maybe this wasn't a series of child abduction cases. But what it could be I'm still uncertain. What I am certain of, these families must be linked somehow by whatever this symbol means. I just hope for the sake of these children that their parents were not involved with their disappearance.

CHAPTER 8

The GPS said that I'm still about twenty minutes out from the Morgan home, and each minute of anticipation is like a nail being driven into my very core. I cannot help but to think of all the things that I could find in this house. What if these people were associated with each other because they sell off their children at a certain age to gain substantial wealth? Like some kind of high society trafficking group. But that doesn't make any sense. The Douglas family is not wealthy by any means. The house was very basic and didn't seem to scream out money to anyone that visits. But it could be a front.

    I was obsessed with the what ifs so much I lost the track of time, I'm here. I pull into the driveway of what seems to be a very nice home. With a house this size, it might be more appropriate to call this a manor rather than a home. Pulling up I could notice a circle drive around a small fountain. It was a floral stone fountain with water spraying from around the middle of it. The house was built of stone, tan in color, and pillars held the front entrance. It was as if I had drove up to a very nice country club and should expect valet service to take my car and park it for me. I started to get out of the vehicle and noticed the drive was made with small ice white stones so clean it resembled snow. I went towards the door, but before I could make the last step to the stairs, I was greeted by some sort of house help, a butler, I presume. He introduced himself to me before continuing to ask why I was there.

"Good afternoon, sir, my name is Corbitt Jenkins. I'm the Morgan's home assistant, or butler, if you prefer. What can I do to assist you?"

"Well, Mr. Jenkins, I'm Detective Hodge of the Louisville Police department, and I'm here to speak with Mr. and Mrs. Morgan about their son's disappearance. I did not get a chance to sit down with them at the station and ask any questions. Are they available to speak?"

I noticed when I mentioned Chris Morgan's disappearance Mr. Jenkins had a reaction that he hid very well. It was as if he was given an order not to react, and rather keep a certain amount of professionalism about him while on the clock.

"Well, sir, Mr. and Mrs. Morgan are not home at this time. But they will be back momentarily. Come on inside and wait for their return, it should not be much longer."

"Thank you, Mr. Jenkins." Mr. Jenkins motioned me to come inside behind him. I followed and before I could get a word out, he motioned me liked a traffic director would cars to come on. He pointed towards the sitting room to the right of the front door. I went into the sitting room and began looking around.

"Detective Hodge, I encourage you not to touch anything while you await their return. This room holds a lot of different antiques from some time ago."

I began to look around, noticing some old glass work on the shelves as well as antique furniture. I don't know too much about antiques, but what I do know is that people pay a ton of money for some of these old trinkets.

It was then I noticed that behind me was another large room with bookshelves on the wall I could see. It must be the room where the family photo they gave us for our file was taken. I need to see that plaque on the wall, but if I do, I'm sure Mr. Jenkins would notice I left this room. It was at that moment he came back in the sitting room where I was.

"Detective, is there anything I can get you to drink while you wait?"

"Do you have a Coke?" I said trying to think of something that would give me just a few minutes to take a look at that plaque in the other room.

"Yes, sir, I will go and fetch you one right away. Do you prefer ice, or would you just like it in the can?"

"I do prefer ice, thank you." I knew that if I could get him to be busy for just a couple of minutes, that I could get into that room across the hall. I watched him walk down the hall and make a right towards what I assumed to be the kitchen. It was in that moment I knew it was now or never to try and see this plaque. I turn around and start towards the other room, and as soon I get out into the hallway, the front door begins to open. I hear voices coming from behind the opening door, it sounded like a man and woman chattering and laughing? It must have been the Morgans, but the laughter surprised me; parents that just filed an abduction case for their only child, it wouldn't seem they would be in such high spirits to be laughing about anything.

I immediately turn around and start looking at whatever possible on the walls I can see, luckily enough there was a family portrait close by that I could pretend to be examining rather than looking like I was wondering the halls.

"Hello, sir, and who might you be?" Mrs. Morgan asked, with a hint of startlement in her voice.

"Hello, Mr. and Mrs. Morgan, My name is Detective Travis Hodge and I'm the lead on your son's abduction case. I apologize to come unannounced, but I hadn't had the chance to meet you earlier when you were at the station and had some questions, I'd like to ask you about the case."

"We have already told everyone down at the station everything we know. I'm not sure what else we can say about it?" Mr. Morgan said resistantly.

"Sir, I apologize, but this won't take too long. I just want to make sure we haven't missed anything. Sometimes when speaking at the station there are things you might have forgotten to mention because of the intensity of the situation."

"Alright, Detective, whatever we can do to help you find our boy, we will comply. I apologize it has just been such an overwhelming experience. We are trying our best to keep it together at the moment."

"I can't say I understand what you are going through, it must be unbearable. But that is exactly why I would like to hear everything from you guys in person, rather read your file over and over." But the real issue isn't the fact I can't read it from the file, I want to know what emotions they show as they are telling it. I want to see for myself that there isn't any possible way they could have anything to do with this.

THE LAST MARK

"Detective, why don't we go into the library over here and sit down. We will tell you everything we know."

Little did they know that's exactly what I wanted to do anyway. I wanted to see what that plaque from the picture was for, and to make sure the symbol was the same as the album from Ms. Douglas's hidden room. We walk in the library and sit down in front of the fireplace.

"Alright, Detective, would you like me to start from the beginning?"

It was at that moment when I sat down that I looked up to where the plaque was in the family photo and noticed it was gone.

"Detective? Is everything alright?" said Mr. Morgan with an underlying tone of conceitedness.

"I'm sorry, yes, I'm fine. Please start from the beginning and try not to miss any details." Mrs. Morgan looked more than less enthused about having to go over these details again, but also it seemed like she was somewhat relieved Mr. Morgan was speaking.

"Detective, we had just gotten home from a dinner we were attending for my firm. I'm the Managing Partner for Morgan & Thompson, and we were throwing a dinner for a year of success. We were late getting home; I would say around eleven o'clock. Corbitt had already put Chris to bed before we arrived. But as always, we had checked on him in his bed quarters. After that we had we went to our room and started getting ready for bed. We had some to drink at the dinner last night. We were in bed by eleven-thirty, I would say. The next morning when my wife had woken up to start her yoga, she had checked on Chris and that's when she noticed he was gone. Darling, why don't you tell him the rest?" Mr. Morgan said, with a sense of cockiness.

"It was like my husband had said, I got up to start my yoga, and when I went to check on Chris, that is when I noticed he was not in his bed quarters. I went downstairs to see if he had just gotten up early and was eating his breakfast. But when I got down to the kitchen, all I found was Corbitt starting preparations for breakfast." Mrs. Morgan said, with exhaustion in her voice.

"Mrs. Morgan, what time would you say it was when you woke up for yoga?"

"I wake up every morning around six o'clock. This morning I would say it was right at six, on account of I woke up a couple minutes before my alarm."

"So, after you had noticed he was not in the kitchen, what did you do next?"

"Detective, I've already told the officers at the station everything about this morning, and I'm very tired." She said, irritably.

"Mrs. Morgan, like I said before, I just need to ask these questions to clarify and see if anything was missed from the earlier statement given."

"Stephanie will tell you everything you need to know, I apologize. She is probably just overwhelmed at the moment and that is clouding her judgement." Mr. Morgan said, interrupting the conversation.

"Yes, you are right. I'm sorry detective I don't know what came over me. After that I had Corbitt go outside and see if Chris was outside playing in the garden, or the tennis court."

"So, what time was it that you knew without a doubt that Chris had gone missing, Mrs. Morgan?"

"It was around seven o'clock this morning. That is when we started getting around to go down to the station."

"Alright, is there anything else you can remember about last night that would seem off?"

"No, it was a typical night, if we came home late. Chris in bed, and we went to sleep shortly after arriving home."

"Alright, may I take a look at his room, Mr. and Mrs. Morgan? I'd like to see if anything sticks out to me."

"Sure thing, Detective, I'll have Corbitt take you up there immediately."

It was at that time Corbett was coming into the room with my Coke I had requested earlier. Almost like he knew not to interrupt the conversation and was waiting for it to end.

"Corbitt, take Detective Hodge up to see Chris's bed quarters. Please help him in any way possible as well." Mr. Morgan said, with a stern voice.

"Right away, sir; please follow me, Detective."

We started heading out of the room and up the stairs. As we were doing so, I couldn't help but notice some of the pictures on the walls. Family members with such high prestige represented with portraits painted by a commissioned artist, I'm sure. We just reached the top of the staircase, that is when I saw the picture that made my heart bump an irregular bump that minute. It appeared to be Mr. Morgan wearing a robe, black with deep red threading for the seams. It wasn't the robe or the colors that had me feeling this way. It was the symbol that laid on the sleeve of it. The same symbol that was on the album in Ms. Douglas's hidden room. The same symbol I saw in the family photo in the case file. It was at that moment Mr.

Jenkins saw me looking at this photo and said "Detective, Chris's room is right through this door. I took a step through the door, and when I did, it was as if I had lost control of my body entirely. Frozen, in my tracks by the sight of something very familiar.

CHAPTER 9

Looking around the room, trying to wrap my head around what I'm seeing. It was as if I had been somehow teleported back into the Douglas home. This room is identical to Austin Douglas's room. From the Pokémon lamp to the exact monster posters on the wall. I can't seem to make any sense of this. I started getting an eerie feeling being in this room. All I knew is I wanted to get out of here, this house, as soon as possible.

I walked over to the window and checked the seal to see if there was any sign of break in, maybe something Forensics had missed. I wanted to make sure it looked as if I were studying the room for any signs missed, because I noticed from the corner of my eye, Mr. Jenkins is standing in the doorway still, watching my every move.

"Well, Mr. Jenkins, I think I have seen all I need to in here." I tried sounding as professional as possible even though really it was like my legs were made of rubber and mind was racing. I was more than uncomfortable, I felt as if I could have stumbled onto something very strange in this house. Maybe it's nothing, and maybe both these boys were just coincidently into the same exact things. But the fact that all these posters and furniture were in the same exact fashion as Austin Douglas's room really had me spooked.

"Very well, Detective, is there anything else I can do to aid you as requested by Mr. Morgan?"

"No, Mr. Jenkins, I don't think that will be necessary, I have seen all I need to. But may I ask you a question?"

"Whatever you need sir. What would you like to know?"

"Did Chris know an Austin Douglas? Were they friends?" As soon as the question came out of my mouth his face lost a little color. Something about it has somehow spooked him. Which leads me to believe he not only knows something, but he was also instructed not to say.

"Detective….I don't believe I've heard that name before within these walls, I apologize. I wish there were more I could tell you, but young Mr. Morgan didn't have many friends."

"Well, Mr. Jenkins, I heard both Mr. and Mrs. Morgan's testimonies, I would like to hear yours. What do you remember about last night.?"

"Well, Detective, the Mr. and Mrs. were out at some party for his firm. They were late getting back, so I instructed young Mr. Morgan to get ready for bed. Made sure he was in tight in his bed quarters and left him to sleep. Then this morning, I remember Mrs. Morgan telling Mr. Morgan that Chris had been missing."

"You overheard them? Or were they in the kitchen where you were prepping for the breakfast meal?"

"They were in the kitchen at that point, Mrs. Morgan had come in there to ask me if I had seen Chris. It was then she requested I go check outside to see if he was playing."

"What did you find when you went outside? Anything to show signs he was taken?"

"No, Detective, if I would have found something like that, I would have said so up front, as well as reported it to the Morgans."

I started getting the sense that these questions were rehearsed with Corbitt Jenkins. The only thing that changed his tone and body language was when I questioned him about Austin Douglas.

"Mr. Jenkins, I appreciate the cooperation I'll be in touch. I can see myself out."

"Detective, I can't let you do that, it's my job to tend to all guests while on property. Please, I'll walk you to your car."

I started for the door from where Mr. Jenkins never moved from the whole time I was in Chris's room. He did not let me out of his sight the whole time I've been in this house. So, I tried making some light conversation while walking out.

"How many acres does the Morgans have here on this property?"

"Mr. Morgan had bought up most land around him at one point, so it kept growing some years back. Currently, I think he is looking at roughly sixteen hundred forty-three acres."

"Wow, Mr. Jenkins, that is a ton of land. How do you know that Chris isn't somewhere out on the land right now?"

"Detective with all due respect, he knows he is not allowed out there, it is dangerous sir. He could get lost or worse."

As he was finishing his response, we were passing that picture again with the robe holding that suspicious symbol on the sleeve.

"Mr. Jenkins, one last question." I interrupted, so he could see the picture I was speaking about. "What is this symbol on Mr. Morgan's robe in this picture mean?" I could see as I mentioned it there was some hesitation with his response.

"Detective Hodge, I have to get dinner preparations started. Maybe the next time you come you can ask Mr. Morgan yourself and have a conversation about it."

Avoiding the question, he kept walking and started towards the door once we reached the bottom of the stairs. "Mr. Jenkins, I appreciate all the help today, where did Mr. and Mrs. Morgan run off to? I would have liked to say thank you to them as well before I head out."

"Detective, I will be more than happy to pass along the message to them. As I am sure they are busy at the moment tending to the calls about Chris. Leave your number for them with me and I'll see to it that they receive it. "

"Alright, Mr. Jenkins, here is my office number, as well as my cell. Please give me a call with any further details you might think of." Corbitt Jenkins took my card and put it into his inner coat pocket. I knew it would more than likely stay in there, especially as it seems he was trying to rid the house of me.

I got into my car and started to drive away. I could see Mr. Jenkins in my rearview mirror watching my car go away from the Morgan residence. As soon as I got to the end of the drive, he started for inside the house. So many questions I'm desperately needing answers to. Like, why did

Chris Morgan's room look identical to Austin Douglas's? Why was the plaque with the symbol taken off the wall, and what was the symbol about? It appeared on Mr. Morgan's portrait along the stairway on the robe worn in it. Why was it that Corbitt Jenkins, the house butler, was avoiding the question about that picture?

The drive back to the office was like I was on autopilot. My highway hypnosis had kicked in, I'm guessing, when I started thinking about all these questions I was having. It had always been so easy for me to lose myself in thought, especially while driving.

I just arrived back at the station, and as I was pulling in, I started to think how late it had gotten. I hadn't realized I was out at the Morgan home for nearly four and half hours. So, I decided on second thought I would grab the files form the station and head home and work from there.

I started for the door to the station and as I was coming in, I had noticed that Chief was not back in his office. Many officers were at their desks doing whatever they can to help with the madness of civilian calls. Wondering what could be done to ensure safety of their children in their homes, mostly mothers were flooding the lines. Of course, the officers on the phones were trying to ensure that their safety is the number one priority and to lock their doors. But anyone could tell you that is just something being told to the people in this community to keep them at bay. The truth is, we aren't sure what to do in this situation, because we were still trying to figure the situation out.

I got the files and started heading home. The drive home was nothing but questions buzzing through my head. Over and over, thinking of what this symbol could mean, so I decided to try and look up any information I could online when I got home. I pulled in the driveway and started heading in the house. I poured a glass of milk and stuck pizza rolls in the microwave. I never grew out of eating pizza rolls; to this day I eat them for a few meals a week. You can't beat how simple they are, and how great after a long day.

I grabbed the plate, my glass of milk, and the files and headed for my desk. I sat down and started eating and flipping through the files. I opened Chris Morgan's again to study that plaque in the picture. When I opened the file, the picture I had just reviewed before speaking with the Morgans was laying on top. Only the plaque with the symbol on it was no longer in the picture at all.

CHAPTER 10

"No, this can't be right! I just saw it this morning before heading to their house! It was clearly in their file; it was the only photo given from this family!" My mind was racing, and I couldn't seem to calm down. Did I just imagine it in the photo? Is that why there wasn't a plaque when I was in their library?

"No! It doesn't make sense; I saw the symbol again in the portrait on the wall of Mr. Morgan. It was on his robe sleeve, and I even questioned Corbitt Jenkins about it!" I was in the house for quite some time, someone could have swapped the photos. As soon as I got done asking Mr. and Mrs. Morgan questions Mr. Jenkins didn't leave my side. It makes sense why he kept a close eye on me, and where I was heading.

So, if they made a swap, it was while I was in Chris Morgan's room. It had to of been then, and they instructed the butler to keep me occupied while they did it. But what tipped them off of doing so? I didn't ask a question about the picture until I was heading out the door. Also, where did they get a photo of it without the plaque? Digitally altered is an option, but they would need time to do it. So, they had to realize they gave us that photo with the plaque holding that symbol on it soon after giving it to us.

But I had shown up unannounced. The Morgan's were surprised to find me in their home. It just doesn't make any sense how they could have pulled this off. "Unless!" Then it hit me, like a bolt of lightning striking an old school television antenna outside during a summer storm. When I was driving out of their private drive, I noticed Mr. Jenkins watching me. He saw as soon as I left their house and must have followed me to the station. He waited until I was inside and went for my car and made the switch then. I can check the security camera and it should show him getting into my vehicle. I grabbed the files and immediately jumped back in the car to head towards the station. I must see the security footage to make sense of all of this. As I'm driving, I had finally put some things together for certain. One, the Morgans have something to do with all of this. Two, it must be something significant they are doing to aid in this crime if they are willing to have their hired help do something like tampering with evidence. This is only a hunch but if I'm right it proves the Morgans are involved significantly in some shape or form.

Pulling into the station I hurry and park my vehicle, lock it, and run inside. As I was entering the building, I noticed it was surprisingly quiet. I head over to the room where we kept the security camera footage and began to start going through it. I focused to the time when I got back, which was around five o'clock and began to play it. I saw myself driving in and watched carefully from there. After I parked, a car drove in behind me. Then suddenly the screen went black for a brief second, and then a hooded figure appeared in the parking lot. It was almost like the tape had a glitch in it, his image jumped and appeared closer. The hood was as dark gray as it could be without being black, and it appeared to be torn. The figure stood almost eight feet tall, and long bulky arms, and slightly tilting its head. Then, there was nothing at all. The camera went black for a moment, after a minute had passed it went back to the regular view. Showing me walking back out to my vehicle.

My hands were shaking, and I started breathing a little heavier. I rolled the tape back trying to see this figure again as much as I couldn't stand the thought. I got to it and paused the footage right on his face when he was the closest. The hood, with nothing but shadow covering where the face should have been. As soon as I started to look closer at the image, the video glitched out and I couldn't get it back. The footage was gone just like that. As if someone cut a portion out of the video.

Still shaking, not understanding what I just saw, I try to rationalize what this could have been. But the more I keep thinking about it, the more I realize this figure is matching exactly what Gerard Glover had described earlier in the day in his testimony. I stood up and looked out into the station, and it was at that moment I noticed I was alone.

CHAPTER 11

My heart beating at a faster pace now, and then the lights started flickering. I backed myself into a wall and started scanning the station in front of me. The lights flickered another time, and in the moment the lights came back, right across the room was the shadowed figure staring right at me. I began to take a step right, and it mimicked my moment. I took another step, and it followed the same. At that moment I stopped and took in a deep breath slowly, and before I could let it out the figure started charging for me.

    I took off running as fast as I could towards the door but could feel it close behind me. I got to the door, opened it, and kept going until I reached my car. I opened the door and got in quickly and locked it right after it closed. Looking out the window towards the direction I came, I saw no one. Scanning each direction around me searching for the figure that just charged me, I saw no one. I tried to catch my breath and calm myself down. At that moment, I started believing Gerard Glover and his testimony.

    Just as I had started to catch my breath, my phone rang. "Hello, this is Detective Hodge."

"Detective, this is Tim Morgan, Corbitt had told me when I returned that you had some more questions for me. Why don't you come back out to the house? We can sit down, and I can answer any further questions you might have."

I knew in my head that this can't be a coincidence him calling right after what just happened. But how could he have anything to do with that thing that just tried charging at me.

"That sounds fine, Mr. Morgan, I'll be out there within the hour." I started to head out towards the Morgan Manor again and tried preparing myself what this evening might hold.

***

As I pulled onto the manor's drive, lit up on both sides by lights following it all the way around the fountain, which was also lit with golden lights making the water shine. I noticed Mr. Jenkins awaiting me at the door. "Detective, welcome back, come on in. You will find Mr. Morgan in the library from before."

Walking in I found Tim Morgan in khaki slacks and a black button up shirt, sipping on what appeared to be bourbon. The fire was lit in the fireplace. It had lit up the room with a waving orange and red tint of color. The fire was cracking, and Mr. Morgan stood up and asked, "Can I get you a glass?"

"Yes, thank you." I was looking up at the wall where the plaque used to hang.

"So, Detective, what was it that you wanted to ask me about?"

"Well, Mr. Morgan, I could use a few questions answered. The first would be that, in the photo you turned into the station there was a plaque hanging on your wall just right over there. It had a symbol on it, and when I came in to ask originally the general questions it wasn't on the wall, nor is it now. What happened to that plaque?"

"Detective, I'm not sure what plaque you're talking about, do you happen to have the photo so I can see it?"

"The plaque I'm talking about actually had the same symbol on it that the portrait on your wall by the staircase had. It was on your robe sleeve."

"Detective, I'm not sure what symbol you're talking about. The portrait on the wall has no symbol on it. Would you like to point it out to me?"

"Yes, let's go take a look at it. I saw it, and immediately asked your butler about it. He told me that I would have to asked you about it personally sometime." So, we began walking towards the stairs to look at the portrait, just knowing I wasn't crazy.

Near the top stairs at this point, I stopped and pointed towards the portrait on the wall. Only when I did I noticed there wasn't a symbol on the arm of the sleeve of Tim Morgan, it was just a robe.

"You see detective, I'm not sure what you were referring to. There isn't a symbol on the sleeve in this portrait. Nothing but me, and a nice robe given to me by my family. Do you have any further questions? Listen let's go take a seat, and you enjoy some of the bourbon I poured you. It tends to help me relax a little bit more.

I knew that I had seen this symbol in here in that

portrait and in the photo given to the station. I don't know how they are pulling this off, but I know what I've seen.

"Detective, are you alright? It's apparent that you are not getting enough sleep." I took the bourbon and drank it like a shot. Maybe, I was imagining parts of this investigation. No evidence whatsoever of this symbol anywhere, except where I found it originally. I must get back over to the Douglas place.

"Mr. Morgan, I have to go, I apologize for any inconvenience. But something has come up."

"Alright, Detective, well you let me know if there is anything else I can do for you. Corbitt, can you show the detective out?"

"I'll show myself out Mr. Morgan." I started for the door and went out to my car. Heading out of the Morgan manor drive I started trying to figure out something that would warrant me coming this late in the night to the Douglas's home to look around. So, I called the chief on my way. After so much ringing I didn't think he would answer, but last minute he did. "Hodge, I was just about to call you. There's been an incident. The Douglas home had a gas leak and burned to the ground. I have Ms. Douglas with me here filling out a testimony."

I felt an overwhelming sense of hopelessness. Every thought I've had has ended up with a dead end, like someone has already thought of it. I know what I saw in the Morgan's photo, and on the portrait of Mr. Morgan. I know for a fact I asked Corbitt Jenkins about it while I was in the Morgan manor. I saw the shadowed figure in the station, and now Chief is telling me he is there right now with Ms. Douglas. I just don't understand this, maybe I haven't had enough sleep.

"Chief, there was something in the Douglas home I thought of that I should go back and try to investigate further. What remains are there of the house?"

"Travis, are you referring to the symbol you found at the Morgan's Residence? You thinking you'd find it at the Douglas house as well?"

"Chief, how did you know about that? I never told you on what I've found yet."

"Travis, why don't you come back to the station, and we will figure all this out?"

"Chief, on second thought, I have some other things I need to look into before coming back to the station."

"Travis, I really think…." I cut off the conversation by hanging up the phone while he was in mid-sentence. There's only one way he could have found out what I saw at the Morgan's and that was by talking to someone in Morgan manor and them informing him. That's when I concluded there was no one I could trust.

CHAPTER 12

I pulled off the rode onto an old turnrow to try and gather myself. Stepping out of the car trying to take a breath of air, I so desperately wanted at this point. I soon realized this January night was a fierce one. The fluorescent moon catching every object around with a smooth surface. Whistling winds breaking through every nook and cranny making an eerie whine. With the wind came a chill that broke through every stitch worn, and temporarily crippling. I had no one... I've been reminded of this many times in my life. But it seemed now more than ever when the odds against me kept piling up. This wasn't the first time I've felt alone, my life has molded me to feel this way for as long as I can remember. But now, children's lives are depending on me being able to overcome.

  It was in that moment that I had remembered one of the first victim's files I had read. Charlie Mitchell, he lived just outside of Parksville, not too far from where I was at. There never was any follow up on this child once we had forensics out there. If I can find another connection, before the Chief or anyone else knows, I may be able to figure out what this all is.

Getting back in the car and starting to head to the Mitchell's house I couldn't help but think what I was going to do when I actually got there. They were probably not going to let someone in at this hour, and if they did, should I trust them anyway? Pressing the pedal with content on the inevitable outcome was the only option I had at this moment. I couldn't let my fear strangle out every ounce of courage I had left. Going down the highway getting closer to the house I tried to spot it. I pass Highway 34 and started to see it coming up on the left. Going off the picture I had in Charlie Mitchell's file.

While slowing down my car and closing in on the distance between me and the house I noticed there were no lights on. There wasn't a single car outside of it anywhere. It seems like no one is at home at all. I pull up next to the house as the driveway connects to it from the side. Getting out of the car, I try to listen for any sound of movement inside. But, after a few minutes of hearing nothing, I started to approach the door.

The house was two stories, with a shallower top floor. I could tell by the size of the windows, comparing them to the ones on the ground level. The door was a darker color, and because of the light of the moon I could see the wood grain detail on it, knots and cross grains showing throughout. The handle looked to be from the original build, which was I'm guessing sometime in the early forties.

I raised my fist to begin knocking, shaking from the cold as well as fear of the unknown. Knocking again in patterns of four, each pound a little harder. After the second time of doing so there still was no answer. I made the choice of reaching for the doorknob and trying to turn it. With much surprise came the rotation of the knob turning…the door was unlocked. I opened the door and called out, "Hello! Their door was open. Mr. and Mrs. Mitchell?" There still wasn't a response. "I'm coming in now!" Treading slowly through the threshold of the house, with my heart breaking through my chest. I knew very little about what I would find in the house, I just knew I had to try and make a connection to figure out what I'm up against.

The house was still, enough to where you could hear a change in the air pressure. The air standing in place, seeing the floating specs of dust reflecting from the moonlight entering in the through the front window. I took out my flashlight, shining it through the door while entering. When walking in, you are immediately looking at the stairs to the upper level, and the small hallway entering in the kitchen sharing that space. To the right, you see what is to be a den, or study. To the left, you see a living space being used for a family room.

Walking through the small hallway leading to the kitchen, I see pictures on a small, thin table. Seeing the couple, but not any pictures of Charlie. I continue into the kitchen, only to find no one in there. The fridge was running, but there wasn't any type of picture or school papers on it.

I turned around and started making my way for the den. Following the wall of the narrow hallway, noticing the white crown molding on the top and bottom of the walls. On the molding were the shapes of shells or maybe fans, surrounded by what appeared to be leaves. Coming to an ending point, I entered the den.

Scanning the flashlight from corner to corner of the room, passing a large black object, an old wood stove. Startling me at first, especially after my encounter earlier on in the evening at the station. Not too far from the stove stood some chairs, and a small end table. Nothing fancy, but probably nice when they were originally made. Those were the only objects in the den, not even a third chair for their child. I started to wonder why there were no signs of a child being in this house at all.

I head back out to the entrance and started to face the stairs. Thinking of what I found in the Douglas home while being there, I made my way up them. Getting to the top of the stairs, looking left was one room, and the right was the other. Each room on the ground level had a room directly above it. I chose to look in the room on the left, and on the outside of the door was a lock. When shining the light, it appeared to be brass. It was the type of lock with a knob on top of a latch, when it moves it meets a connector on the door frame. But why have the lock on the outside of the door, other than to keep someone in? I started moving the latch and opening the door. Shining the light inside the room, it began to reflect off what appears to be chain and restraints.

While walking into the room I was overwhelmed by the smell of ammonia, and some type of acid. Something you might smell being inside of the emergency room, filled with soiled linens and filled gag pans. Shining the light on the floor under the restraints I could see stains from where someone had been relieving themselves and getting sick. Getting closer to the chain and using the light I could see the leftover residue of skin and blood from the where they had it so tight on whoever wore them. There was nothing else in this room, like a holding cell for a dangerous criminal. There was no way that a forensics team came in this house and didn't find this room. This whole thing had to be staged and meant to look as if there were kids being abducted. But these people look like they have abducted someone else's child and held them in here for days on end, to the point of dehydration and having to relief themselves where they were chained.

I went across the hall and went into where I assumed the adults were staying. The dresser lined with a woman's jewelry collection, as well as a man's comb and cologne. Simple, but very neat. The bed was perfectly made like in a magazine. White comforter and sheets, and end tables on each side with nothing on them. Simplistic, and complete opposite of what was across the hall. I went over to the closet and opened the door. When I did, the first thing I saw in the back hanging side by side were dark red robes with black stitching with the symbol I saw on the album from the Douglas home and in the portrait in the Morgan home. This was it, the connection I needed. These people are all apart of some group, or maybe some kind of cult.

Losing air again and trying to breathe, I manage to get out of the closet and head towards the staircase. Taking the first few steps down were hard as my legs were shaking. Looking up and shining my light towards the door, it slams shut. "No!" taking the stairs down at a faster pace I reach the door and can't get it open. I immediately turn around and start shining the light towards the stairs and hallway to the kitchen. I start hurrying towards the living room, looking out the window seeing if I saw anyone in the front of the house. No one was there; I turn around and start back towards the kitchen, looking for another way out.

I get down the narrow hall, and when I opened the door, it was like someone had pulled me back by the back of my collar on my shirt and slammed me onto the floor. Air leaving my body on contact, I struggle to find my footing. I manage to get back up on my feet, and when I turn around, I see it. The dark figure staring straight at me, hand out towards me. I backed up to the kitchen, knocking over what little pictures were on the small table. Taking steps towards me consistently as I'm backing away, I began to shout. "WHAT DO YOU WANT!" I was still backing away but losing space to go to.

Suddenly the door opens, "What the Hell are you doing in our home!" The Mitchells had just gotten home. The figure had disappeared right in front of me as soon as they opened the door.

"I'm Detective Hodge, and we need to get out of here!" Stepping towards me, the husband looks furious. Then the shadowed figure appeared behind them. Before I could even give warning, he raised his hands behind each of them and grabbed their necks. Within an instant I heard a sharp snap. Leaving both of their heads in such a state they were laying back touching in-between their shoulder blades. Blood had started to seep from their eyes, mouth, and ears. Dropping the bodies to its sides, it started coming straight for me. Then I started hearing a commotion outside the home; neighbors had heard the screaming and came over. People were gathering outside, as the noise got louder, the figure was no longer in front of me.

The neighbors had come up to the door, and the woman let out a blood curdling scream. "WHAT HAVE YOU DONE!" The husband moving towards me, looking to restrain me.

"I'm Detective Hodge of the Danville Police department. I was here following up on the investigation for their child!"

The neighbors saw one thing, the dead bodies of Mr. and Mrs. Mitchell. They didn't know me, they knew them. At least, they thought they did. I'm sure they had no idea about how they treated their child. But at that moment, it didn't matter. I had to run, get out of here. Someone would have called the police by now, and that means Chief Smith and the Morgans would know where I was.

I bolted for the door, knocking over both neighbors who had got in my way. I turned my head as I was running and apologized. I got in my car, put the keys in the ignition and turned it, hit the gas pedal, and got out of there as fast as I could. Driving trying to not get noticed too much, I didn't know where I was going to go. I didn't have any options. The Danville Police department knew where I lived, so they would show up anytime, if they weren't already there. Was I actually safe anywhere I went with that thing after me and these people against me? A dark and wrenching pain of anxiety fell over what sane mind I had left at this point. I had no idea what, why or how. I didn't even know why "it," or they were taking the children. But I would be damned if I were to let these children die.

Getting close to the edge of Danville, trying to figure my next move. On the road that connects Danville, like most small towns have, I start noticing no one was anywhere in sight. Shop lights were all off, restaurants all dark. Even the motels on the side of the road had no one in their parking lot. I stop at a traffic signal blinking red. In smaller towns this is common for intersections so people can stop and go whenever possible. As I was sitting there, I notice the streetlights starting to flicker one by one. Knowing what follows the lights flicker, just like at the station, I slammed the gas pedal and took off. Looking back in the rearview mirror, I see it, the figure, standing in the middle of the road.

Hands starting to sweat, making gripping the wheel difficult. My breath beginning to shallow and taking in more air frequently. Looking back at the road lying before me, I start to wonder if I was going to make it through the night. Then the startling noise of classic phone ringing started. I was getting a call, but from an unknown number. Hesitant to answer, for the simple fact that it could be the Danville Police department trying to trace my call. But I had no other options, if I was going to help these children, I needed to explore what was in front of me.

I answer the phone and before saying anything, a woman on the other end said "Meet me off Highway 1896, where it meets Mocks Branch Creek. I can help you." Just like that the woman hung up the phone. There were only two things I could do: go and see if this woman is actually trying to help me, or keep running and try to outrun some creature and a group of people against me.

Mustering up enough courage to make the turn north of town, I started making my way to the meeting point. Knowing that this was probably a set-up, I kept heading towards that direction.

On the highway the woman specified, I started looking for markers, or signs of water. Slowing down, I see a small bridge and next to it going down the bank is a path. Broken down grass to the dirt from where people have been walking over it. I pull off the road and park on the side, almost to the point you think the car would tip over and roll. I grab the flashlight and crawl over the console to get out the passenger side. The driver side door was in a position where I would have to push it up and climb out, I decided the passenger was best. I close the door and turn the flashlight on. I start scanning the area around me, nervously thinking that whatever that creature was would find me once again. But, at this point what other choice is there but to push forward?

I take the path down to where the creek meets the bridge. I start scanning with the light all around me, until when the light meets the face of someone standing under the bridge. Jumping at the sight of the face of the woman, that's when Mrs. Morgan said, "I'm glad you came, Detective, there is a lot I need to tell you."

CHAPTER 13

"Mrs. Morgan, I can't trust you. I sat in front of your earlier today and you lied to my face. WHAT HAS HAPPENED CHRIS? WHATS HAPPENED TO ALL THESE CHILDREN!"

"Travis... this town has darker secrets than I think you've realized. Secrets that will damn us to where we belong. I've been a part of terrible, horrific things. I can't take back the things I done acting out from my own fear. But I owe it to your mother to tell you the truth."

"This is another lie, to lure me to your husband. To all of them, for WHATEVER this is. I never had a mother!"

"Travis, you did have a mother, she was my closest friend growing up. She was an amazing woman, that cared for everyone. Gracie-Anne Hodge, we grew up right down the road from here. We would come down here to the creek every day each summer. We had an old tree house about a quarter mile up the hill there, into the woods."

"How can I believe a word you're saying? I have people after me, including your husband. I don't even know why! I've had some creature from Hell after me, almost taking my life TWICE tonight! Why would I believe a single word you spew through your teeth!"

"Travis... you have a birth mark on your arm. That wasn't there by chance. That birth mark was there by a choice your parents made. Have you seen that mark on the other children that have fallen victim to this?"

"What are you saying...?" Barely getting the words out of my mouth. Knowing what she was going to say was horrific, but then it began to snow. The cold breeze slammed into my eyes as I couldn't close them from fear and disbelief. Drying them out made blinking nearly impossible.

"Your mother and father had gotten into something deep, much like the rest of our town. Out of desperation, the group convinced him to do what he did."

"What group, Mrs. Morgan? Why did my parents abandon me?"

"Travis, your mother had fallen very ill. She was diagnosed with stage four leukemia. That's when your father was then approached by my husband, Tim, and was convinced to join the Disciples of Moloch."

"The Disciples of what? My mother was that sick, so what would joining some cult do for them?"

"The Disciples of Moloch, followers or worshipers to a dark deity or demon that will grant what they need or wish for the promise of their first born. The parents agree to giving up their child at the age of ten, and that's when Moloch himself will come and take the child. But what makes the mark significant is that when the parents agree to this, the parents at birth notice a mark given to the child making it nearly impossible to escape. Moloch's mark is a part of him; that's why he can manipulate what he needs to get the child he has been promised. But your mother didn't know about the deal he made to save her until she was already healed, and it was too late. Once she found out, she and your father had gotten you far away from this place in hopes for your safety, to live a full life, out of harm. But, in the works of trying to hide the fact that they did that, they returned to Danville. When they did, the word of your absence got out and Moloch.... brutally killed both of them."

Not knowing what to say or how to feel, I tried to stay on the task at hand. "What does Moloch want with all of these children? Where are they now?"

"He needs them to survive. Once the child has been taken, he has his followers sacrifice them in his name by burning them alive."

"You people handed over your children to a demon, just to buy yourself more time? How many others are there? How many in this town know about this?"

"They are still alive, that's why I'm here. Travis, I want to help, I want to try and save my son. All of these children!"

"HOW MANY IN THIS TOWN KNOW, STEPHANIE?"

"…. There isn't many that don't. Moloch came to a town that was struck not only by sickness, but dark times. All the others were killed, the elderly that had nothing to offer and the others that had everything they needed. He made it seem like it was accidents, but I know differently. You probably heard over the phone about the Douglas house?"

"Yes, the chief was telling me right before trying to get me to come into the station."

"Travis, you knew it wasn't an accident. Moloch found out that you were closing in on discovering the Disciples.

After you asked about the symbol on the portrait, he knew you had to have seen it from the Douglas home. What he didn't know is that I gave the photo with the plaque on the wall to help you."

"Mrs. Morgan, where are the children now? How will we get to them without being noticed?"

"They are kept on the backside of our property in a large old stable. But it won't be us going to help the children, it will have to be you alone. I can't be gone that long without Tim noticing I'm missing."

"How am I supposed to find this barn on my own, and go undetected to help the children?"

"I've drawn you a map that will tell you where to head through our property to find yourself at the stable. While you are finding your way there, I plan to be trying to keep my husband occupied. I'll do whatever is necessary to keep them off your trail while getting there. There isn't anything else I can do for you."

"Moloch has found me everywhere I have been, how will he not see me coming a mile away!"

"Travis, I know it seems impossible. But your mother got you all the way to Indiana without him detecting it. I know you can do this; I see your mother in your eyes…"

Mrs. Morgan walked away, leaving small footprints behind her in the snow that had fallen. Light crunching noises with each step she took. Watching her as she peaks the bank side, an overwhelming feeling began to set in.

My father, even though trying to save the love of his life, my mother, was willing to sacrifice his first child to a demon. Knowing that one day, that demon would come and take his child and have them killed. My mother not knowing about it and being so upset about his actions, that she got herself and my father killed trying to get me to safety.

All this time, I thought my parents had abandoned me because they didn't want me. But it was really my mother trying to save my life. I had someone that loved me enough to give her own life to keep me alive. For the first time in my life, I felt that I had someone. That I wasn't truly alone.

CHAPTER 14

The snow had been falling for some time now and had covered the tracks left by Mrs. Morgan when she left. Cold air blew through the tall dead weeds around the banks made a wisping noise you might hear from a traditional style broom and the subtle sound of the water, only freezing over a thin layer next to banks as the rest kept moving were all I could hear now.

My next moves from here are very unclear, the only thing I kept thinking was how much time those children were out in the old stable, how cold they must be, and if some of them were even still alive. I couldn't bear the thought of it.

I rolled up the map given to me tighter to fit in my pocket. Starting to make way to the car, I'm climbed up the bank. The snow crunched under my feet, dampening out most other noises. Each step sounding an alarm for any animal that was nearby to move on or hide and that someone was coming.

Getting to the top of the bank I look back at my car, and notice the snow build up in a short period of time on the roof and hood. But the windshield, and rear window barely covered as it had remained warm from the heat being on while I was driving here. I use my hand and pushed off the little bit of snow on the windshield and got in the car. Cupping my hands and trying to warm them with a single hot breath, I noticed was just making them damp from the vapor.

I started the car, turned the heat on, and then I turn the reading lamp on and gaze at this map given to me. Looking at the layout of the Morgan's property, I noticed there are many places where the children could be hidden, but Mrs. Morgan had made it clear which stable on the property was the one the children were in when she outlined the shape on the map in darker black ink.

I started to head to the Morgan's property, then realized I need to try and get to my house. I can't go in there unprepared. I need to at least carry a few weapons. But I knew the house would be watched, there's no way I'd get in there right now. Suddenly, that sense of hopelessness came back to me when realizing, I'm going into this with barely anything.

I drove down the road, seeing the faded yellow lines dive under the driver side bottom of the car. As cold as I had been, my anxiety had started to cause me to sweat. Air feeling so vacant in my car, gasping for more than just a second or two of air at a time began to be quite difficult. This was type of air that couldn't barely be fixed with a burst of Flovent. But what was there to be done right now other than to try and slow my breathing? This isn't going to stop, not until those kids were safe and I didn't have to look over my shoulder every turn. I grasped the steering wheel harder than I had in a while and just took in a deep breath. It was twenty seconds later that I let out a scream from my body I didn't know was capable of me, screaming at the dash from frustration, anxiety, helplessness, and then anger.

The drive was going to take me awhile longer than just going to the Morgan's house, due to me having to drive back roads to the opposite end of their property. The time in the car thinking of every possible negative outcome possible was bearing down on me.

I look down at my phone to find that there wasn't signal anymore. But, earlier today in this very part of town, I had signal. Right then, I started to hear a slight whisper. A voice so deep, that it made the hairs on the back of my neck become erect.

"Travis… you have nowhere to run I can't find you… this will end, and you will be mine. Your life taken… like it was promised to me. I won't let you get away again…"

I pulled off to the side of the road I was on in a state of mental hysteria. I've never heard that voice before, not until now. If he could have found me, then why was I safe all these years? My mind slipping from reality into a deep consciousness of unknown and fear. I wasn't sure what to do from here. He is speaking to me without seeing me. I can't go undetected to help these children, it wasn't possible with Moloch near me. I need to find out more, whatever information possible would help.

I put the car back into drive and made a U-turn, "Kids, I swear I'll be back to get you. He won't get away with what he's done." Thinking of places that I may have seen that maybe I can find more information, or anything. The library may have something, or I can even see if anything was left from the Douglas home in that rubble. Anything would help right now, even if it's just the history of where he came from.

Just then I thought, my mother had to have figured something out. That's how she was able to get me out of town, far enough I was safe all those years. Something had to of given the idea to do that. But I have no idea where they lived while they were here. Plus, would she have kept any information they found in the house where the other disciples could find it? "The treehouse!" It was in that moment I had remembered what Mrs. Morgan was telling me about their childhood. That they had a tree house about a quarter mile from where we met earlier. It's a long shot, but what other ideas really make sense right now?

Heading towards the meeting point I was just at earlier; I began to ask myself if Mrs. Morgan would have thought about checking there? But she wasn't looking for an answer on what my mother had found, but more along the lines of how she could help me without being caught. I can't imagine what would happen to her, if Mr. Morgan and or Moloch had found out she had helped me. I tried to stay focused because I couldn't stand the thought of someone else dying to help me.

I see the sign reflecting in my headlights. As I got closer and the reflection of my headlights became brighter, I looked away from how bright it was. It was in that instant I switched my focus up to the rearview mirror to avoid the bright glare of the lights. When I did, I saw a figure, the demon sitting in my back seat staring back at me. Eyes made of pits, fiery orange, and yellow, and deep black ovals in the center. The rest of the head lighting up in a flash as the reflection from the sign was passing, black skin, short black fur covering its face, and the horns of what appeared to be a taurus sticking out from each side of the head. I swerved the car and turned my head around to find nothing in my back seat. Finding control of the car again, I made the turn onto eighteen ninety-six.

Seeing where I pulled off the road the last time, I passed it and continued to drive just a little further. Mrs. Morgan said a quarter mile this way, so to make the distance back to my car as short as possible I pulled off right at a quarter mile mark on my odometer.

Pulling off the road was more difficult than the last time from all the snow. My tires slipped as I turned them slowly in the deep snow, noticing a small skid when breaking. I put the car in park and grabbed the flashlight. I had to hurry; it wouldn't be long until someone found me.

I started making my way up the side of the hill, almost bringing my knees up to my chest with every step. The drifts on the side of the hill were large and becoming difficult to move through. Finally shallowing out towards the top of the hill, I began to walk normally. I looked each way trying to locate the treehouse, scanning the flashlight through the trees as a watch tower would do when someone would escape a prison.

It was then I saw a brief glimpse of what appeared to be a wood ladder hanging on a tree down the way from me. Making my way towards it, moving my flashlight up and down trying to see the treehouse itself still. Getting closer to the ladder, I started to see what appeared to be walls for it above me. Getting directly under it now, looking at the flooring to see if it could still withstand my weight. I put one foot on the first step and tried applying some of my weight to test it out. I climbed up slowly, trying to be careful with the many years of rot and decay this structure had seen. Looking closer at the wood and materials used for it, seeing the weathering. Small cracks spreading throughout the grains, that cracked with each step I applied.

Getting to the top of the ladder now, peeking my head up through the entry point for it. I climbed inside and peered my flashlight through the darkness that overwhelmed this old children's get away. Going top to bottom and from side to side, on the walls were old pictures, looking to be drawn by young girls. One that stuck out was of two little girls holding hands, with "BEST FRIENDS FOREVUR" above them colored in blue crayon, then followed by the one on the right saying, "NO BOYS ALLOWED."

Following the wall art to the opposite side of the treehouse, I found a cabinet. I opened one side of it to find an old board game in a dilapidated box, where all the corners of the lid were torn to the seam. Next to it a jar filled with what looked to be metal marbles, maybe ball bearings. The jar read, AMMO, sitting adjacent to a sling shot. Apparently, my mother and Stephanie Morgan were prepared for whatever kind of trouble came their way back in the day.

Continuing to look through the cabinet I saw some miscellaneous items such as hair pins, some old chewing gum balls in a bag, as well as an old tin lunch box. I grabbed the lunch box and pulled it to the edge of the shelf and unlatched the two metal locks on it. Opening it up, I found an old picture of what I'm guessing would be my mother and Mrs. Morgan. Shining the light on the old picture, I saw them standing side by side in front of a beautiful two-story house. It was yellow in color with white shutters on each side of every window, a white wrap-around porch, and a white front door. Turning the photo over, a label for the photo was written. "GRACIE-ANNE AND STEPHANIE WILLOW, AUGUST 2ND, 1979."

I stuck the picture into my pants pocket and keeping looking through the treehouse in hopes to find something. Then looking down next to the cabinet I see a small hook, made from a bent finishing nail. Hanging on it was an old backpack. I unzip the bag and find an old notebook and a doll. Opening the notebook, I notice at the top right hand of the page was my mother's name next to her grade and classroom number. It was a one-page autobiography written for class. It started with, "Hi, I'm Gracie-Anne and I'm ten years old. I have a mom and dad and we live in a yellow house down by Mocks Branch."

It was then I had put two and two together, the house in the photograph was my mother's old house. Looking through the backpack further, I didn't find really anything. But when I was closing it up, I noticed on the back a name tag. It read GRACIE-ANNE EVANS, 426 HWY 1896, DANVILLE, KY.

Immediately, I started to think that I haven't found anything in here showing evidence of any information my mother may have found on Moloch. But, knowing in that picture was the house my mother grew up in, it could be possible it is where she kept the information she had found. The address showing it is down the road a bit, but still within just a minute or two from here.

I took the backpack and the photo that I had put into my pocket and started to head down the ladder. Reaching the bottom, I began to point the flashlight in the path I was starting to head. Shining the light, the snow began sparkling with each step taken. The woods were quiet, still, as if someone had muted the volume of the world around me for a moment. At the bottom of the bank now near my car, I began making the incline. When I got back to my car, I put the backpack in the passenger seat and put my seat belt on, as the road looked to have gotten worse since I had arrived back at Mocks Branch.

I put the heat on and put the car in drive. I started looking for mailboxes to find the address number. Shortly after starting to move down the highway, I see the first mailbox, it showed, "388 Wheeley." I wasn't too far off from where I was wanting to be. I drove another couple of minutes and another mailbox had appeared reading, "400 Lesley." Another few mailboxes came after, reading, "410 Smith, 416 Klein, and 422 Fehr." Watching for the next one as it should be the one, I'm looking for, I see another mailbox coming up. The mailbox read, "426 Evans." This was it, the house that could hold answers to things I'm needing to know. The information my mother had gotten to save my life.

I start turning my wheel slowly to make the turn, trying my best to keep my car from drifting in the snow. Going down the driveway, I noticed the weeds were grown up tall on both sides, around three foot taller than the snow. Going up and over a small hill, I see the house, a faded yellow color with cracked and some broken white shutters. The house looked to be neglected for some time now. To the right of the house was an older looking barn with a lean-to built off the left side. Under it looked to be a late eighties model F-150 that was white and popped tires all around. Getting closer to the house's front porch, I park and get out of the car. I grab the flashlight again and shine it up to the house. The windows were covered in dust, and the front door showed cracks in the paint as I was getting closer. The front porch looked to be still in good shape as I walk up the steps and head towards the door.

I reached for the doorknob to find it was locked. Desperate for the answers I could find in here, I walk back down the steps to the driveway and grab a large rock. Taking the rock back up to the door, I broke the glass on it, and reached for the handle on the inside to unlock it. As soon as I opened the door, a horrid smell aggressively rushed towards my face. The scent made my eyes water, with high contents of fecal matter and rancidity. Like walking into an animal shelter that was left uncleaned while the animals have been there. But the rancid smell was as if someone had left raw steaks outside in the sun, and then brought them in. The air in this house being so dissonant from what is outside was a shock to my sinuses that it burned with every little gasp of air I took. It was then after I took a breath, I held it and heard a very faint noise. One which sounded to be like someone stirring a bowl of wet noodles. I needed to find the smell, and the source of that noise...

CHAPTER 15

My flashlight was scanning in front of me as I was entering the house. Immediately to the left was a room, and a staircase to the second floor. To the right was where the house had opened to a large living area connected to a kitchen that had a large wooden table and benches on both sides for dining. The walls are white, and the kitchen had a printed white with lemon wallpaper. The layer of dust had invaded the furniture and walls, so thick you could probably make an indention with your finger when doing the typical one-finger swipe you see on television shows.

The flooring looked to be the original from when it was built, nice hardwood floors with a lighter, almost caramel color. The furniture in the living area were all a forest green color. The couch cushions uneven from one side being so worn that it sunk into the frame. But the other looking to be almost untouched and new.

There were two chairs in front of the couch, and a coffee table in between. The two chairs were the same forest green as the couch, only there was a floral print on top of that green as well. All so covered in dust you could hardly tell what they had on them.

Immediately turning left, I open the door at the foot of the stairs. Glancing inside I saw it looked to be a bedroom, possibly for a guest as it was incredibly bare. A wooden bed, made with a quilt and two pillows. There weren't any kind of nightstands, but there was a lamp in the far back corner sitting on a smaller desk. A shallow closet not too far from where the desk was. An accordion style door on it and was open and empty. Going back out of the room and towards the kitchen I heard a subtle humming noise. I froze and started shining my flashlight all around the room. My heart started racing again, thinking Moloch could have found me already. Shining my light in the direction from where it came and when I did, no one was there.

I continued towards the kitchen, flashlight reflecting off the icebox's chrome handle. It was an older one that was white, with the latch on the front. Looking over to the left there was a gas stove, and an old wooden box, it read, "Potatoes," on the front of it. The box was in good condition for being how old it is. Standing still, admiring this old kitchen storage I could hear the sound again. I started heading in the direction of it, turning around seeing a door to the right of me. It was on the far side of the kitchen and led outside. But right next to it was another door that was cracked open, looking to be going down to a basement.

Walking towards the door slowly, I try listening for the noise again. I could hear it louder than before; it sounded like it was coming from down there. I was so hesitant to push the door the rest of the way open, not knowing what could be making that noise. The smell grew stronger with each step, enough to where it was getting close to having a reaction out of my gag reflex.

Opening the door further, I focused the light down into the basement. It was then I saw movement on the floor, tens of thousands of small worms, maggots, crawling over a pool of bodies that had been dumped. Flies buzzing around, thousands of them, explaining the humming I was hearing from the other room. Shining the light, some of the bodies appeared to be more recent killings. The skin was mostly intact for some, near the staircase, while others had been slowly devoured and decomposed over time. Bones exposed from the rib cages as well as limbs on some, and other not so recently killed victims filled with holes from where the maggots had run their course, enough to make anyone's tropophobia come to surface.

To the far back of the room, I see a wooden work bench with three leather straps. One on the far left of the bench, and two adjacent from each other halfway down it. The was bench soaked red from where the victims' lives were taken from them.

I started walking down the stairs to better examine what has been going on in here. At the end of the staircase, I see a light switch, which I then reached for and flipped on. As soon as I did, looking back farther into the basement, the sea of bodies that lay on the floor was visible, and overwhelming. It's more bodies than I've ever seen in one place, more than any other crime scene I've witnessed or read about.

Someone had to of been using this house since my mother and or her parents have had it. It had to have been some of the cult members that had been using this space.

Using the Disciples of Moloch for justification for the murder they have been wanting to commit. This had to of been more than one person doing this as well, there was too many bodies for one person to accumulate. I look to the right of me on the floor next to the stairs is a cardboard box, opened with one lip hanging out to the side. Looking down at it a little bit closer I could see a small fragment of light reflecting off something inside of it. I reach down and take ahold of the lip on the opposite end of the other. Opening it I began to see what has been going on here… Reaching down into the box I pull up what was appearing to make that small amount of reflection. It was a driver's license for a man out of Alabama. By the birthdate listed on the license it, he is only twenty-nine. Looking back down to the box, I reach in and pull out a handful of them. Driver's licenses from multiple different people, men, and women alike. It was then I began to see the full picture. These were trophies, probably from all these people down here. I put them back in the box and put the lip of the box back in the state I found it.

Turning back around to head towards the bench, I notice now with the lights on, a large peg board fastened to the wall. Holding multiple knives, hammers, and even saws. This bench was more than just somewhere to kill the victims, it was a chop shop, built for humans. I'm not sure what kind of monster could do all of this. The pure evil it would take to desecrate and mutilate so many helpless people. As I was getting closer to the bench, I notice the marks on the sides from where the nails of the victims had tried clawing their way out of captivity, a last desperate attempt to try and save themselves. But how desperate the marks look, how frantic, it doesn't appear that anyone was successful.

Turning my head away from it, as it was too much to bear, I look towards another wall to the right of the bench. That's when I see it, the symbol of the Disciples of Moloch, drawn in the blood of these victims on the wall. That's when I heard a voice call out, "We done saw your car parked out front. Come on out and play, I'm sorry we weren't home when y'all got here. Me and my brother are back now, and we'd love to meet you!"

I immediately started looking for a place to hide. I knew they would know I'm here because my car had been parked out front, but if I can get the chance to just get up the stairs to the door leading outside in the kitchen, I had a chance.

"Don't be shy now, we love us some company. We've had tons of company. Just come on out now."

"My brother and me love making friends, do you want to be our friend?"

I went to the bench and grabbed a small blade, and quietly dashed over to a large mound of bodies in the back of the basement. Trying to overcome the smell, and the thought, I started moving some so I could squeeze myself into the pile to hide. I got half of my body covered up, and that's when I heard a footstep hit the first stair in the staircase. I hurried and pulled another body over the top of me and tried breathing as shallowly has possible. My body was shaking from the fear of these backwoods' brothers finding me, as well as the maggots that began crawling on me from the bodies on top. One of the maggots started inching its way on to my face. Trying to hold it together, and not make a noise that's when I saw them.

Through the small gap between the body's arm on top of me and of the one next to me I could see them walking down the stairs looking out over the bodies that have piled up. One of the men, about six foot three, white, and eyes sunken in. He was wearing light-colored blue jeans, lace-up boots, and a camouflage jacket. His hair so nappy and skin so greasy, it looked as if he hadn't showered in weeks.

His brother had darker colored blue jeans, a white t-shirt, a black zip-up coat, and square toe cowboy boots.

"Now, Earl, I don't see nobody down here, where did that detective run off to? You know Moloch won't be happy if he finds out we done let him get away. He might not let us have our fun no more."

"Don't worry Charlie, we'll find 'em. Ole Detective probably just hid upstairs in one of them rooms, go on and look for 'em."

"Earl what about our new friend out in the truck, I don't wanna to let him miss out on the fun."

"Ok Charlie I'll find that there detective, why don't you goes and get our new friend from the truck."

"Okay, Earl, I'll grab him right quick." He started walking back up the stairs, and his brother started for the pegboard. He grabbed a large knife and started heading in the direction I was hiding.

Looking around some garbage they had piled up along the walls, filtering through it looking for me, Earl said, "Come on out boy, I know you're in here somewhere. I'm gonna find ya before too long. When I do I promise I'll treat ya real nice like." Getting closer to where I was, I started getting the knife ready. He was just a few feet from me now, bending over to look by a mound of bodies next to me. He straightened his back and started looking my direction. As he was bending down his brother started down the stairs and yelled out to him. "Earl, I got him, but he's squirming a lot now."

"Be careful, Charlie, we want to have fun with him, if you drop him down them stairs, we won't get no chance to!"

"I'm sorry Earl, I won't drop him."

Seeing his brother struggling he straightened back up and started to head over towards him to help. He grabbed his feet to help his brother, and they laid him up on the bench. As they started to strap him in, that's when I saw that it was Gerard Glover! The witness that had seen Moloch in the night and came and made a testimony.

"Well, hey there, Mr. Glover, Moloch said we were allowed to have our fun with you cause you been causing some trouble, telling that detective about him and such."

These men were going to kill him, I had to think fast on how I would do this. I had to get their attention off him long enough for me to make a move. But I know for a fact I wouldn't be able to take the two of them. But then I had an idea, I started reaching into my pocket for my car keys. Feeling around on the key fob, I was able to hit the panic button on them, causing the alarm to start blaring.

"Charlie, go check that out, don't you dare let that detective get away now, ya hear?!"

"I'm on it Earl, don't start without me!" He grabbed a knife and started up the stairs.

The other brother focused back on Gerard Glover and started running his blade along his skin. "Mr. Glover, I don't think my brother would mind if we do a little bit while he's gone do you?" Gerard tried desperately to get loose from the rope they had him bonded with.

While his attention was on Mr. Glover, I slowly started moving the body off me. Going as slowly as possible, but still with enough haste to try and do something. I get the body off to the side, and slowly stand up. Creeping as quietly as I could over to where the brother was standing over Mr. Glover. Only a few feet away, I slowly raise my hand up that is holding the small blade I had grabbed. Swinging it with full force, stabbing the side of the brother's neck. The blade was fully submerged, I put my other hand on his head, and remove the blade. Blood had poured profusely from the wound and made it very difficult for him to talk. Gargling on the blood in his throat as he was trying to scream, he choked and couldn't make a noise. At that moment, I took the blade and ran it directly across the front of his neck, causing him to immediately drop to the floor.

I started to undo the restraints on Mr. Glover and told him to remain quiet. "Gerard, we need to make our way up the stairs and out the door at the top, leading us outside. But you need to stay quiet and move fast." Mr. Glover nodded his head with understanding and followed me towards the stairs. But as we got to the foot of the stairs, the other brother was looking down at us and saw his brother lying dead on the floor.

"Earl!! WHAT HAVE YOU DONE TO MY BROTHER! EARL, GO ON SAY SOMETHING TO ME!" Charging down the steps, we take a step back and I push Mr. Glover out of the way. The brother came at me attempting to thrust his knife into my chest. I grabbed his hand before it made contact and started pushing against it. He grabbed me, forcing me backwards, and onto a mound of bodies. His face so greasy and sweat pouring from his pores. His eyes of a darker brown color and dilated. His neck pulsed from a large vein popping out on the right side. He wanted nothing more than to feel that blade filet my body, especially after finding his brother dead on the floor.

Stabbing at me, just barely missing, and piercing the bodies of the victims underneath me. Each one making an awful, hollowed hitting noise as the knife went into the lifeless bodies. But then suddenly I feel a warm sensation on the bottom right side of me. I look down and notice that I had been impaled with his blade, enough that it had caused the blood to soak up that part of my shirt. I hadn't felt any pain from the wound until I saw it. But struggling to hold this guy from putting that knife into my chest, I guess I hadn't noticed.

I called out to Mr. Glover to help, but he was frozen in fear. "Gerard, help me!" He slowly got up to his feet, and while visibly shaking, grabbed a ball-peen hammer from the peg board behind the bench. Fumbling the hammer in his hands, Mr. Glover raised it above his head and brought it down directly on top of the brother's skull. When striking the head, the hammer made a large crack from the bone shattering from contact. The brother began to turn his head around in response, but as soon as Mr. Glover saw him make a move, he struck him again in the forehead, then the cheek, and then the jaw repeatedly. The remains of the brother's face were blundered and sunken in, making him unrecognizable. His eye socket forced inward from the blow and the jaw broken in what appeared to be two pieces.

His forehead had been split severely, and the skin severed and left with a groove. His body dropped onto the floor, making a sound that I won't be able to forget. Not only did it make the thud as it hit the floor, but also the sound of more bones being broken as it hit.

I couldn't move for a few minutes following this, but I could manage to get a few words out. Looking at the bodies that we had added to this place, that we were personally responsible for, my stomach began to churn. I tried to justify this situation but simply failed in doing so. This was the first person I've had to kill in my career. I've never had to end someone's life in a gun fight, or even in self-defense, not until tonight. I immediately started to dry-heave. Not eating for a few hours now, nothing came up. But the sheer thought of someone's life being stripped from them by my hands made me sick to my core.

"Detective, I don't know what would have happened to me if you wouldn't have helped me. Putting yourself in harm's way. You saved my life…"

Trying to catch my breath, I hold one hand up to him to show him I need a second. "And you saved mine, we are even. But we need to leave, others will come. Did you hear them say anything while you were captive?"

"I did hear some things; I know that they were to get rid of me. They said it was because I told you what I witnessed about Austin Douglas going missing."

"Who was it that told them to get rid of you? Does the name Moloch sound familiar?"

"I'm not sure, Detective, I was in and out from when they got me. I was hit over the head and gagged. What's going on?"

"Gerard, have you ever heard of the Disciples of Moloch?"

"I can't say that I have…"

"Well let me tell you, it's a cult filled with the people of your town. It is to worship Moloch, and sacrifice to him. In return, he is promising to care for the needs of the people. All the children missing, including Austin Douglas, were agreed to be given to him on their tenth birthday. Moloch needs them to survive, and if I can't find a way to help them, the children will be burned alive as tribute to him."

Gerard Glover was speechless, and as a few moments went by I could see in his face the anger arising. "Detective, what do I need to do to help?"

"We need to get out of here first, then we can figure that out." I grabbed his arm, as he attempted to help prop me up to walk. Then the lights in the basement started to flicker. "We need to run Gerard!"

"Detective… look…"

Looking over to our left, lights flickering we see one of the brother's bodies stand up and facing our direction, not making a sound, and standing very still. We started to realize the mounds of bodies piled high by these backwoods maniacs were beginning to move as well. One by one standing up, bones and limbs falling from the decayed bodies, yet still able to move. The bodies all in an up-right position, moving their heads all towards our direction. The eyes immediately popping open revealing the eyes of evil I had witnessed in the car earlier in the rearview mirror. These were the eyes of Moloch, in all of them. Slowly backing up to the stairs, the group of bodies started to move closer. The corpses began to move slowly towards us, jittering with each moment of the limbs.

"RUN!" Heading up the staircase, I turn to find the bodies that had risen starting to make a faster pace towards us. There in the back of the basement, behind the bodies stood the shadowed figure, Moloch. Getting to the top of the staircase, we take the door immediately to our right, and went outside. Running to my car, feeling a sharp, excruciating pain with every step, we make it inside the vehicle. Not caring about the seatbelt at this moment, I put the car in drive and spun the car around. Going as fast as I could down the driveway, I could see in the rearview mirror nothing but the tracks we had left. Turning my attention back to the road, I made the turn out of the driveway and fishtailed the car a bit. I was able to straighten it up just in time before hitting the opposite side of the road.

"Detective, what was that....? Who was that? How is this possible...?"

"Gerard... that was Moloch. He is after me, and because you are still alive, he will now be after you too."

"Detective, I see lights behind us in the distance." As soon as I heard that, I focused my attention to the rearview mirror where I began to think that it wouldn't be long before the others got word. I still wasn't sure how many people in Danville were involved, but what I do know is, we were being hunted.

CHAPTER 16

"Gerard, are you familiar with this area? I need to know where to go."

"Keep going straight down this road, when you come to the bridge, take an immediate right after crossing it, I have an idea of where we can go."

I wasn't feeling very confident of Mr. Glover's idea of a place to go, even before he told me. I knew that it wouldn't be long before the others caught up to us, and Moloch was right back on our trail. The slight ray of hope these children had of being saved was growing very dim.

"It will need to be somewhere they don't know about already. It can't be your house, or something like that."

"I understand, I was grabbed from my house. That's the last place I plan on going. But, right outside the East of town, where Mocks meets Dix River, I have some land out there with a hunting cabin. It fits right in between where the river bends, forming an isolated island. Right at the peak, there is a bridge I built years ago to cross with a vehicle."

I didn't want to say it aloud, but I know it won't be long until they find us there. Even if we could lose the mind washed idiots behind us. Not to mention, I need to be trying to figure out a way to rescue those children. But when I got close to where they were…. he not only sensed me coming, but he was also able make his way into my mind. Who knows what else he is capable of? My options are dwindling away, and I'm not sure what I can do about it.

"Detective, take a right here! There is a road not far from here that we can lose them on!"

Turning the wheel, and trying to keep the car on the road, I notice the car starting to drift to the left. Quickly I let off the break and gave it some gas to straighten us out. The car started to gain some more traction, and when it did, we kept going. With that turn we should put some distance between us and the horde of cars after us.

"Right up here we should see a sign for Highway 32. When we hit that, we are going to take it down three miles until we see the County Road 668 sign. When we hit that road, we follow it all the way to the end."

"Do you see any of the cars behind us yet? The snow is pretty rough on this road, I can't take my eyes off it."

"No, Detective, we're still good. I don't even see the headlights yet. But we need to hurry. If we can hit the highway before they turn, we should lose them."

As that was said, we peaked up over a hill. As soon as we peaked the top, I could see the highway from there. It looked to be no more than a few hundred yards from where we were. "We will make it, if we can survive the house we were just in, we can lose these people!"

We reached the highway and started to make the turn, but the eerie part of it all was that we hadn't seen the headlights of the disciples following us. The possibility of the disciples not being the headlights we saw is slim to none. But either way, we should have seen some type of light behind us by now.

"Here's the county road, Detective, turn here. Now just follow this all the way to the end."

Trying to hurry, but still fighting the wheel to keep the car under control. "These gravel roads are awful in the snow. I'm barely able to keep the car in the middle of the road." But truthfully it wasn't just the road being made of gravel, it was the fact the snow has started to freeze to the road.

"The road should end just up ahead detective. There will be a small path, just big enough for a car to fit through. We will take that, then you'll see the cabin soon after that."

"Do you think we will be able to get back in there with the snow how it is?"

"Yeah, we should be alright. Just be careful. There is some water on both sides of the path halfway down it. Like I said, the island there is in between the river fold."

Getting to the end of the road I started to slow down, I could see the pathway he was talking about was guarded by a large bulge of snow. I eased my way up and was barely able to get the car over it. Immediately after we heard the rear bumper and exhaust scrape the ledge covered in snow, we eased along the path and I could see the pines on both sides draping over the ground, burdened with the weight of the snow on their branches. In the wind, watching the branches brush against the snow, almost like they were making their own type of snow angel.

The water was visible now, I could see us coming up on it. I started to slow down a bit more and to try and not go off into it. Creeping across the small pathway that connected the mainland to the island peak. I started to feel a small sort of relief as I noticed the back tires had passed the last section near the water. I just knew that if we would have gotten the car stuck, we would have been sitting ducks.

"There's the cabin, Detective, just pull up right next to the porch. We should be okay now, at least for a while."

He was right, we hadn't seen any more cars following us and if no one knew he had this place out here, I can't see how we could be found quickly. I still wasn't sure of what Moloch was capable of. But, for the time being we can at least warm up and figure out a plan.

Getting out of the car, I started to really get a good look at the cabin. It was very small and reminded me of the old log blocks I would play with as a child. It was a single-story cabin, with a front porch. The chimney was towering up the right side of the place and was made of grey stone. The roof on top was made of tin, and green in color. Each log used for the cabin had a round end sticking out of the sides of each wall. There were two windows on the front of the cabin, and one on the side. The wood was a dark color, and the logs had some type of vine growing up the sides. The moon was bright and had made it very easy to see those details of the cabin.

Heading inside, I noticed Gerard reaching for a light switch. "It's not much light, but the lamp will at least keep you from hitting your head on something."

After turning on the light I saw Gerard go to the back of the cabin and got into his version of a firedog. The split wood was stored inside it. He grabbed a few pieces and began to start the fire in the fireplace. Grabbing a box of matches and an old newspaper, he planned to use as easy kindling, he stuffed the newspaper underneath the split wood and sparked the match. After doing so, he reached over to the old cast-iron stoker holder and grabbed an old bellow. Grabbed both handles of it and began pumping in air to the fire to keep it going. After about fifteen minutes, he was finally able to get it steady.

With the fire burning I was able to see so much more in the cabin. The fireplace was made of an old grey stone. Each stone lined with an off grey grout connecting it all. There were pictures on the hearth, some of catches Gerard has had over the years, and an old reel he used to catch them with. Something you would expect to see in a hunting cabin.

The walls were the same logs as seen outside, only without the weathering to them. The ceiling was covered in cobwebs higher up, as it had a high pitch. The living room was connected to the kitchen in one open area, with one bedroom off to the side. There were two chairs in the living room, both a dark red color that reminded me of a barn.

On the kitchen side of the room, it was bare. The kitchen table was just a cheap wood, two chair table like you might see at an apartment of a college student. But I suppose for a hunting cabin someone barely visits, it would be feasible. Besides the table, the kitchen only had a small one door fridge, and a three-burner stove, both white in color.

"Detective, we need to get your wound taken care of. I have a first aid kit in the bathroom, give me just a second to grab it." As he was in the other room, I started to lift my shirt to see just how bad the damage was. When I did, I could see that I would need stitches. The stab wound was around three inches long and was bruised surrounding the puncture point. It looked like a wound from an old war movie. I wasn't used to seeing myself bleeding this much, it almost comes as a shock seeing yourself like this. Until you are hurt, you start getting a sense of invulnerability to the world, just because it isn't a part of the norm.

"I got it detective, I have some gauze, and cleaning solution."

"Gerard, I'm going to need stitches. Do you have any thread?"

"I don't have anything thread, Detective, but I have some thin fishing line. I know it has been used in other countries as medical sutures, I'm sure we can make it work. I'll grab a new hook as well from my tackle."

The thought of a fishing hook being used to weave my skin like an old basket made my skin crawl. But right now, I wasn't sure what else can be done. If I bled out, I wouldn't be able to help the children, or us in our situation for that matter.

"Okay detective, I'll sterilize the line and hook with alcohol first. Then we will see what we can do here."

He doused the fishing line and hook with rubbing alcohol and started to make a knot with the line around the hook. That's when he gave me a rag and motioned me to bite down on it.

"Detective, I'm going to clean the wound first." Taking a bottle of hydrogen peroxide and dumping it over the stab wound. It bubbled on contact, and I winced in pure pain. Biting on the rag hard enough I thought my teeth would break out of my gums. That's when he grabbed the hook and line, pinched together the stab wound, and started to weave the line in and out of my side. Each stab of the hook hurt more than the last.

"Detective, I'm sitting here stitching you up and can't help but wonder why you never pulled your firearm at the house. You had a knife out, risking your life so much more than you would have if you just used your weapon. Why didn't you use it?"

"I know it's going to sound strange, Gerard, but I have never liked guns. Since I can remember I never had the fascination that other boys grow up with for guns. I became a good marksman in the academy, but as soon as I passed, I never went back to using it."

"All the time on the force and you have never used a gun, or even been in a fire fight? That sounds pretty fortunate, but foolish to not trust in your skills of the weapon."

"It isn't that I don't trust my capabilities with the firearm, it's the gun itself. Taking someone's life isn't something I take lightly. I've used my gun as intimidation, but I rarely keep the clip in it. Which in the worst-case scenario I guess could have ended up badly? But the truth is, I don't find it necessary to achieve what I want in a situation."

"Well, in this situation with all these people you call the 'Disciples' after us, we might consider getting your firearm loaded. We might need it to make it out of this alive. I have an older hunting rifle here, it's my old Marlin 336 lever action. I should have the 30-30 rounds it needs as well. So, even if you don't decide to use your firearm, I'll have my rifle."

"Well, I appreciate your support, OW!"

"Alright, you're all fixed up detective." As he finished the stitching Gerard had pulled the line tight, causing a sharp pain to shoot through my side. It started hurting every big breath I took, and movement I made. "I think I might have some Old Forester Bourbon in the cabinet, you can use it for pain."

Gerard went and grabbed the bottle and two glasses from the cabinet. Poured me one, and before he could sit, I had it down and asked for another. "I'm a Jameson man myself, but right now anything will do."

"Ahhh Irish whiskey, it does go down smooth. But there's something about Kentucky bourbon that just reminds me of a summer evening. So, I tend to stick with it and Old Forester is one of my favorites."

"Either way, I appreciate it. The pain is terrible, and anything I can do to help it pass is great. But I did want to ask you something as well."

"Well, Detective, go ahead and ask away. It's not like we are going anywhere for at least a little while."

"Mr. Glover, how is it that you have lived in Danville so long and aren't apart of all of this? You had to have been approached by someone about it. Mr. Morgan has approached almost everyone in this town, knowing their weakness and what they needed desperately. That's how he has been able to convince them they need the Disciples of Moloch. Don't you have a family or children?"

"No, Detective, I never found the right woman for me. Earlier you said that Moloch was needing the children to survive, maybe that's why he never came to me? I didn't have anything for him to want."

"It just doesn't make sense, then I thought he would have killed you by now. WAIT! Can you think of anyone else in this county that is single with no children!"

"Well, I know a few people from church that are single with no children. But I'm not sure where they would live."

"Gerard, I can use my cell to look up the names you come up with. Maybe it's possible there are more people out here that can help us."

"Alright let me get a pencil and some paper, I'll start writing down the names of the people I know."

Gerard found a pad of paper and a pen and began jotting down all the names of people he knew that were single it didn't have any kids.

"Detective, I think I have a pretty decent list here of some people that would be what we are looking for."

I stood up, and as soon as I did a sharp pain shot up my spine from the wound. It made me a little lite headed where I felt like I could faint. After a few moments of my vision being fuzzy and the colors had stop floating in front of my face, I was able to focus on grabbing the list.

Picking it up I began to read the names he had come up with.

Peggy Strout
Robert Knoll
Elijah Crow

Only three people, but this list is better than none. I pull out my phone and immediately started plugging the names in to search. Typing the name P-e-g-g-y S-t-r-o-u-d into the search bar, and the first thing that popped up from the search was she was listed on a dating website. I show Gerard the phone so he could identify her picture, and when he saw her, he nodded giving me the confirmation that was who we were looking for.

"Gerard, write this down for me 270-999-0666, that's the number listed on her profile. Now, if I type this number in and put her name with it as well, we might get a hit from somewhere."

I put in the information, and nothing was popping up for me, I knew it was a small chance, but I had to try.

"Alright, we have a phone number. Have you seen any of these people lately?"

"No, actually Peggy, and Elijah are the only ones I've seen in the last year. The others are just ones I know about."

"Alright, then let's focus on these two right now."

I started typing in E-l-i-j-a-h C-r-o-w, after I hit enter there wasn't any images that popped up. Just the Yellow Pages link for the phone number and address.

"Write this number down for me Gerard, 859-344-9966. His address is 1128 Highway 37."

"Alright, Detective, we've got it. What is it you want to do? I don't think we can just come right out and ask if they are a part of some evil group, or cult."

"No, we will go and visit Elijah, and try calling Peggy. You will talk with them, one on the phone, and one at their house. We can try and explain in person better than we can over the phone. But, with Peggy the phone call is all we got."

"What about Robert Knoll? Don't you think we should try him as well?"

"Yes Gerard, I'll look him up right now." I immediately started typing his name to the search bar. R-o-b-e-r-t K-n-o-l-l. I hit the enter on the search button, and nothing. Not a single thing about him, not even social media. The only thing that was offered was a side question, *"Did you mean Robert Toll?"*

"Nothing is coming up for Robert Knoll, do you have any idea where he could live Gerard?"

"I have no idea, but at least we have Peggy and Elijah still. That's better than nothing right?" I didn't respond, and to be honest I wasn't sure if it was enough to just have two other people we could try and get to help us. I'm just not sure of much anymore.

"Detective do you think it's a good idea trying to go Elijah's house? I mean, won't there be people looking for us on the highway we just came from?"

"What else can we do? We can't just sit and wait to die? Those people that are looking for us and they aren't going to just stop. Eventually, Moloch will find us and give them the order to come here and kill us. Not to mention, we would be trapped here on the island. We can't cross the other side in a car, the entry we came in is the only one."

"I understand, Detective, this is just easier said than done. We must get back out to Highway 32. Then once we get there, we have to make our way down it eight miles without being noticed."

"I understand the risk… but I have to try anything to free those kids. I've been given the location; I just need to be able to get there. The more help I can get the better. Do you think we can get in the door at Elijah's place?"

"Detective, Elijah is a trustworthy man, he just has some quirks that can make him off putting. He is a doomsday prepper and believes God has told him when the end will come. But he is a good honest man that would help anyone in need. I'm sure we can get into see him."

"Then, that settles it, we will leave as soon you have your ammo, and rifle ready." I immediately started wrapping my waist with the bandages. But loosely so the stitches could still breathe. I got my shirt back on and went to the window. As I was looking out the window, I saw a pair of headlights coming down the path.

"Gerard, we have company! Grab your rifle and get set up!"

He grabbed the rifle and loaded the bullets. Pulled the lever down to get a bullet in the chamber and got to a window.

"Detective, put out the fire!"

While I was grabbing the bucket of water left by the fireplace, Gerard was flipping the light switch. He got low and to the bottom corner of the window aiming out at the vehicle.

"Stay down, Detective, they are pulling up now. If I can get a shot off and take out one from the get-go, we will have a better shot at this."

Gerard aiming down the scope that he had put on his rifle and whispered, "As soon as your head clears the top of your car door, you're mine."

I was standing up against the wall, next to the fireplace where the stone was sticking out. It ended up being the perfect amount of coverage for me. I peeked my head out to see them getting out of the car, and as soon as I did Gerard fired the first bullet. It shot straight through the window and hit the driver. The bullet pierced through his right eye socket, passing straight through his head. Small fragments of the back of his skull were caused to disgorge, followed by a mist of blood that had carried the reflection of the moonlight. Immediately after his body fell, hitting the door of the car on the way down.

"One down, and one left. He is charging the house! Detective, be ready!"

Running over to the door, and jamming my right foot into the bottom, while holding it shut with my weight.

"Is he armed, Gerard!"

As soon as he was able to answer bullets started shooting towards the cabin. One shooting through the window, and another through the wall next to it. Multiple shots were being fired now, entering everywhere. "Hit the floor, Gerard!"

Getting down low to the floor, him on his back aiming up at the door. I was on my back as well, with my feet ready to kick the door back shut when he tried to open it.

"Still think you don't need the firearm!" I could understand where he's coming from. We wouldn't be in such a tight spot if I would have had the clip on my person and not in the glovebox of my car.

BAM! The man slammed into the door, and I kicked it right back shut. That's when Gerard came and got behind the door, aiming down the sights. CRACK! The man slammed into the door again, followed by me kicking it shut with my feet a final time. As soon as I did, that's when Gerard fired his rifle through the door. It was silent, there wasn't any more movement. Suddenly we hear a loud thud. We opened the door to find the man had been shot through the chest and fell dead onto the porch.

Gerard sank to the floor holding his rifle in one hand, and his face in the other. While trying to catch a breath he managed to mumble the words, "Well, at least there are two less idiots on our trail."

I suddenly had the thought that they could have called or radioed out to others to let them know we are here. I went out the door and came up on the driver that was lying face first on the ground, I saw the massive hole that laid in-between his ears.

I turned around and looked in the car and didn't see a radio. So, I bent down and checked the pockets of the driver. Pulling out his phone, I started checking his call history, there wasn't any sign of communication in the last two hours.

"Gerard, check the phone of the man on the porch!"

Struggling to get to his feet, he managed to stand and walk over to the man's body. Stooping over and reaching into the pockets, he didn't find anything.

"He's clean, Detective, there isn't a phone on this one."

As relieved as that makes me, I'm still feeling unsettled. Something just feels off. When we killed the backwoods brothers, their bodies were turned into puppets. We need to dispose of them, I won't make the same mistake again.

"Gather some firewood Gerard, we need to burn the bodies. We can't risk them standing back up and getting us while our backs are turned."

Mr. Glover didn't respond but instead stared at me with eyes that looked as if someone had stolen whatever ounce of spirit was left in him. He started heading over to the firedog and grabbed all the wood he could hold. He took it over to the bank of the river and started stacking it in a solid form. Reaching into his pocket he pulled out some paper I'm guessing that was left from the kindling he used in the fireplace. He stuck it under the wood and struck a match. Lighting the end of the paper, it started to burn. Meanwhile I was getting the driver and dragging him over to the fire.

Gerard came over and grabbed the feet of the man and helped me carry him. Getting next to the fire, we laid his body on top. After doing so, without a word Gerard started walking over to the second man and grabbed his hands and began to drag. Trying to offer the same curtesy, I grabbed the feet of the man, and we repeated the same motion.
    Standing there watching the fire burn, I felt nothing but numb. The smell of the bodies burning, and the methane byproducts releasing from the organs of the deceased being scorched was horrid. Yet, we still found ourselves motionless, and unable to make a sound.

CHAPTER 17

It seemed like an hour had passed, but realistically it was more like twenty-five minutes. There's a point where returning to a normal life after tragedy is next to impossible. That point can be taking another person's life, or it can even be as simple as your spouse cheating on you, or the other way around. It's when you know there has been a change made inside you, voluntarily or involuntarily. Taking a person's life was something I had dreaded my entire life as a cop. But it wasn't just a couple of hours ago now, that I was surrounded by countless victims, and I added to that count by my own hand. It was that it was getting easier, and that unsettled me.

"Detective, we should probably start heading over to Elijah's house. We need all the help we can get. We were lucky that they came in a pair, the next time we might not get so lucky."

"I'm sorry…What else do we need to grab from the cabin for you?"

"Let me grab the ammo from in there and we can leave."

Gerard ran inside and grabbed the box of ammo and ran back out without even closing the door. But I guess after the door and the window being shot through, it didn't really matter. If someone wanted to go in, they could with ease.

We both were getting back in the car now; I turned the key and saw the gas light come on. "We are low on gas; we need to siphon what gas they had. I'll pull up next to their tank, and you grab a hose."

I pulled the car around to the other side of their vehicle, facing the opposite way, so the gas tanks could be side by side. I got out to help and saw Gerard coming back around the corner of the cabin with an old garden hose.

"Go ahead and put one end of the hose in their tank and give me the other."

I grabbed the end he gave me and stretched it out a bit so there wouldn't be any kinks. I got close to our tank and put that end of the hose in my mouth. Creating enough suction, I could hear the gasoline coming up the hose towards my end. It reached my mouth and I shoved it down into our tank, as well as, spit the excess gas out of my mouth and into the grass.

"Detective, I'd like you to tell me more about this situation. I want to know how you are involved, and what exactly they are wanting from you."

"When this all started happening, my father and mother were going through some difficult times. My mother was diagnosed with Leukemia, and my father couldn't stand the thought of losing her. About that time, Mr. Morgan approached my father and said he knew a way to help my mother. That all her pain wouldn't be taken from her, and she would live to grow old. My father, like any other man, wanted to know how. Mr. Morgan then was able to convince my dad that by joining the Disciples of

Moloch, he could make that happen for her. It wasn't long until my father was told the Moloch would need something in return. That offering their son, on his tenth birthday was what he needed. My father not knowing me, or even knowing my mother would become pregnant agreed. Then after I was born, a mark appeared on my left arm."

Pulling up my sleeve, I showed Gerard the mark, he started to look at it with horror. He was at a loss for words.

"This mark means I was given to Moloch as sacrifice for the fortunes he gave my parents. But my mother finally found out what he had done. She was furious and horrified. She began researching and trying to find a way to keep me safe from him. They ended up taking me to Terre Haute, Indiana. I grew up in foster care and was never adopted. It wasn't until recently that I secretly met with Mrs. Morgan, that I found out about my parents and what happened, as well as all my mother had done to try and save me. But in the end, Moloch still found me. He had one of the Disciples reach out to me online and offer me a promotion to move down to Danville. I was able to confirm this thought when I called Police Chief Smith earlier and he was trying to lure me down to the station."

"...I'm at a loss for words, Detective."

"But the best part was, that I was able to find out from Mrs. Morgan where Moloch has the children kept for the sacrifice. But, when I tried to get out there to them, I started hearing his voice in my head. Moloch was able to have some kind of mental connection to me, where I couldn't do anything to get him away."

"It sounds like that's all the gas we are going to get from their tank."

Saying all of that out loud, hearing those words as they came from my mouth made the situation hit in a different way than it had before. Clarity came in many different forms, but in this case, it was from an auditory perspective. One that I didn't care for much but needed to happen. The last thing I need is to stray away from the reality of the situation at hand.

I pulled the end of the hose out and rolled it up. Putting it in the truck after that in case we get into the same situation later.

"Alright, let's go. We need to go before someone notices those two are no longer responding to communication."

Not a glimmer of relief, or peace came from what just happened, especially for Gerard. It was as if killing them wasn't a problem because it was out of self-defense. But when it came to making sure the bodies weren't going to come after us from the Afterlife, that was something of another realm. But I understand, it wasn't something anyone should have to do.

"Detective, when you get out to Highway 32, take a left. We will follow it down about eight miles or so."

"Let me know when we get close to his road and keep watch for more headlights from behind us." He nodded his head, so I knew he would do anything he needed to from here on out.

After that agreement was made, we got into the car, and I put it in drive. I pulled the car around in front of the cabin and started driving out the pathway.

Tires squeaked and crunched from coming down on the snow as we plunged through it. The pathway only somewhat dark, as the white of the snow had partially lit the way. The moonlight broke up the shadow of the leaves of the trees around. But the most unfortunate part of the night was how beautiful it truly was outside, but soiled with the blood, deceit, and morbid intentions of the people after us.

Passing over the small ledge to the road, I hear the car scraping again while climbing over it. With a loud crack from the tailpipe coming off the ledge and hitting the gravel, we were on our way. Driving at a decent pace I knew it wouldn't be long until we reached the highway. Passing what seemed to be never ending trees on both sides of us and fearing people from the cult appearing out of them. I felt a sense of Xylophobia, or the fear of the woods. Really, I think it comes down to just a fear of the dark, or what's in it. Especially when right now, there was something in it, and it's after us.

I could see the highway coming up, and started to slow down the car, just in case I couldn't stop it in time. My luck is that we would have been through all of this, had to take the lives of other men, and then we slide into the highway and a tractor trailer slams into the car, killing the both of us. So, instead of that happening I decided to press the breaks early, ensuring we stop.

Coming to a stop, I began starting to turn the wheel left, as instructed. From the corner of my eye, I see Mr. Glover peering out the back window, and all around us.

"I don't see anything, Detective."

Starting down the highway, I suddenly had a chill shoot down my spine. It may be just from the blood loss, but with everything going on I couldn't be certain. Looking more attentively out at the road, just waiting for something to happen. But a few more minutes pass and there was nothing.

"Detective, we need to turn right up here on the left."

I could see the mailbox for the driveway he was talking about. It wasn't a street, but a private drive leading to Elijah's house. Slowing down to make the turn, I start looking up the drive towards the place. That's when I see just a small amount of smoke coming from behind the trees down the way. "Do you see the smoke?"

"Yeah, I see it. He could have just had the fireplace going."

But getting closer to the house of the man Gerard once knew as Elijah we immediately were struck by the smell of smoke, and the dark reality that his house has been reduced to rubble and ash. Pulling up in front of the home, we park the car and get out.

Gerard running towards the scorched debris yelling out, "Elijah! Say something if you can hear me!" But there was no response. Getting closer, something had stopped Gerard in his tracks. He was looking down on the ground in front of him.

I ran up to where he was and immediately recognized the horror. On the ground, still smoldering was the symbol of the Disciples of Moloch. On each point of the symbol, laid a scorched and dismembered piece of what we assumed used to be Elijah. Carefully placed at the center of this gruesome pyre to Moloch, was the remains of his head. We were too late....

CHAPTER 18

"AGHHHHHHHHHH" Gerard screamed with every fiber in his being, mentally taken and depleted of all hope and understanding. The frustration seeping with every tear dropping down his face. "WE CAN'T LET THESE PEOPLE GET AWAY WITH THIS!"

"I understand, Gerard, and that's exactly why we have to stay focused. I can't make this seem any less horrible than it is, but I can tell you we have to keep pushing forward. If we don't, this will end up happening to all those children, including Austin Douglas. You said that he used to help you out around the yard and was a good kid. Well, that same kid is facing the same morbid death if we can't find a way to get them out."

Mr. Glover wiping his face with anger, trying to get ahold of himself looks over at me with sincerity. "I said I would do whatever I could to help, and I meant it. We will save those children, even if it means killing every last one of those brain-washed idiots."

The pain and determination behind his words were strong enough they struck my entire being. Engulfed with a sense of companionship, it ignited a fiery confidence. "Yeah, we will. Now, let's call Peggy and see what we can find out."

The next on our list, Peggy Strout, was a woman in her late thirties, and desperate for love. Saturating a dating website with the ideal man for herself. Her profile photo being one of herself holding a coffee cup reading "Blessed," and just beginning to sip it while looking up at a camera. In the bottom right of the frame was a bright orange pumpkin, complimenting her beige sweater. A typical kind of photo for someone wanting others to notice she might be single, but she is content with it. So, she doesn't need to settle for anything less than amazing.

I pulled the piece of paper I had written the names and information on and pulled my phone out to type in the number. I hand the phone over to Gerard, and he waited for an answer. "Hello, Peggy? Yeah, this is Gerard Glover from church. I'm not sure if you remember me much, but I would like to sit down and talk to you a moment." He went silent a moment; I'm assuming while she was responding to such a random request.

"I have a detective here, and he was wanting to get ahold of you to ask a few questions about the recent child abductions. Would that be, okay? I told him I would get ahold of you, on account of us being somewhat familiar with each other from church."

Another few moments of silence had passed, and then, "Yes, that would be fine, I can stop by here in the next half hour. Thank you for your time."

"Where are we going Gerard?"

"She is currently at work, she works at Jenny's, the diner at the southside of town. She said we can come by on her break, plus with all the other people there it might be a safer place to meet right?"

Looking at him giving a small smile with a nod, but in all honesty, I had a lot of doubts. After what happened in the station earlier tonight, I just don't know. But he has the right idea. We can't afford not to at least try.

Getting back into the car, hesitating to put it into reverse, I began to get an astounding amount of pressure in my head. I lean my head back onto the headrest, and then close my eyes. Breathing heavy, just trying to let it pass. Then I open my eyes… finding myself outside of a large stable like barn. The moon shining bright against the pale red grains of shiplap wrapping the building. I hear a faint sound of metal chains clacking against each other. I start easing my way towards the building, and that's when I hear the voices of children. Hearing the desperate attempts to cry out from the dehydrated and worn voices of the small victims. The door crept open before I ever touched it, allowing the moonlight to illuminate their situation. Slowly starting to reveal inside, the children chained to posts inside all the equine stalls. Their wrists bleeding from attempting to wiggle and pull out of the shackles given to them. Eyes surrounded by the dark circles given to them by the anxiety filled nights wondering if they would live to see morning. Their lips were dry, cracked, and dehydrated to a light pink as if they hadn't had a drink in a couple of days.

"I'm going to get you guys out of here!"

The children didn't move their heads, they couldn't hear or see me. That's when men started coming in and unlocking their shackles and began dragging them out. The boys kicking and trying anything they could to be set free from the grasps of these them. But it made no difference, and they were all taken away.

As soon as the door the men drug them out of closed with a loud latching noise, I found myself somewhere else. I was in the middle of a field, in a clearing made amongst tall wheat. There was a large monument made to Moloch, towering over the area. The statue stood about fourteen foot tall and resembling his image with every edge and point. Ominous and dark with horns on both sides of the head. The face not as large as a bull, but still was stocky. Laying out before the statue was a large stone structure, built with a large space underneath the flooring. It had an opening on one side, and the bottom black from soot. It was then I realized what it was…. This was an open-aired pyre that the children are locked in, while a large fire is lit underneath where they are burned alive.

In that split second, I suddenly see the flames engulfing around the kids, while they were screaming for help. The Disciples around the pyre chanting and circling the children. I start running towards them, desperate to help in whatever way possible. While running, I trip from a rut in the dirt of the field. Falling harshly and hitting my head. It was then I was back in my car, looking out the front windshield. My forehead sweating and hands shaking. For a moment I was trapped in a thought, or possibly in a vision of the future. I wasn't sure, but it was so real. I could feel the heat of the flames searing the at the bottom of the pin holding those children. My body overtaken by anxiety and fear, not knowing what to do next.

"Detective! What is it? Are you okay?" But I couldn't answer. My lungs were vacant of air, as I'm struggling to catch my breath. I drag both hands down my face to wipe away the tears, while trying to pull myself together. If we don't hurry, we will be too late. Those children will be incinerated in the name of Moloch, and I can't let it happen. I can't stand by and waste time! I put the car in reverse, whip the car around and started out of the driveway.

"You tell me where to go, Gerard, we need to see if Peggy will listen to us. I'm not sure what just happened to me, but I saw the children. I saw them and the place they are being held. I saw them being dragged out of the stable, kicking and clawing to fight back. I saw them put inside this large stone structure to be burned alive. I heard their screams; I felt the flame. We can't let this happen!"

Gerard looking at me with disbelief, but at the same time nodding. It was a lot to try and believe, I'm not even sure how it can be true.

"Take a left onto the highway, and we will follow it to the south edge of town. The diner is pretty much on the city limit line."

I gave him a nod and kept driving at a decent pace. Hoping Peggy will believe what we are about to tell her, and not think we are "End of the World" people. But it really is a lot to ask of someone to just believe you, especially when that someone barely knows you. I can't say that I'm very enthusiastic about this meeting.

Driving what seems to be for a while now, I start seeing signs for the end of Danville. That's when I saw the sign for the diner coming up on the left. It read Jen's, as one (n) was out, and the (y) was out.

The diner itself looked safe enough, and the people inside were about typical what you would see in a place open so late. I could see one man in a black t-shirt and trucker hat enjoying some French toast. Then there was another older gentleman, wearing an old mechanic jacket with Jake sewed on the patch. He was having some coffee and biscuits and gravy. In the booth right behind him was a couple in the forties, and they were both in jeans and a plaid button up shirts. They were sharing a slice of pie à la mode.

I parked the car, and grabbed my clip from the glove box, knowing I wouldn't make the mistake of being defenseless again. Putting the clip into the gun, and hearing the snap from it attaching, I chambered a shell. We both then start to head towards the door. Gerard entered first, and immediately started looking around for Peggy. She sees us from across the diner and motions us to sit down. We grabbed the booth that was closest to us, and she came over with hot coffee. We weren't here for the food or coffee, but right now it really sounded nice to have a hot cup of anything.

"Hey, Gerard, how have you been? I can sit down with you here in about 20 minutes. That's when I'll be on break."

"That's sounds great and thank you for the coffee. We could really use something hot right now."

"Well, of course, do you guys need something to eat? We have fresh pie, and biscuits just came out of the oven. We have about anything you could want."

I haven't eaten since yesterday morning, and I could really use something. But I wasn't going to get anything unless Gerard specifically asked for food.

"Yeah Peggy, some eggs and biscuits would be great. Detective, do you want anything?"

"Some eggs and sausage would be great. Thank you, ma'am."

"Alright guys, I'll have it out for you in just a few minutes. You guys just warm up a bit with the coffee."

I began sipping on the coffee, trying to get past the initial swallow of the serrated liquid. It was the first drink of anything I've had since the last time I ate, making the first sip stiff.

I see Gerard taking a drink and closing his eyes, getting lost in a moment of serenity. He removes his glasses, puts his hand on his face and breathes in deeply.

"Alright guys, here is your eggs and sausage, detective, and Gerard, here is your biscuits and eggs. Now what is it you are wanting to talk to me about?"

"Ms. Strout, why don't you go ahead and sit down. I'll explain everything, but you need to know this will all be hard to believe at first."

"Okay.... what exactly is going on?"

"Ma'am, we have reason to believe that your life may be in danger. I was informed that you are a single woman, with no children. Is that correct?"

She nods with confusion, and a slightly disturbed face. "Are you familiar with the children being abducted in the area?"

"Yes, but like you said, I have no children; how does this involve me?"

"Ma'am your current situation and life choice fits the personal 'want list' of a certain group of people terrorizing this area. The group calls themselves, 'The Disciples of Moloch.' And we believe they are involved with the child abductions. They find people in a rough spot in life, whether desperate for money, or sickness, whatever that they can convince the victims that the group is needed."

"A cult? There's a cult in little Danville? I hardly believe that all this is happening in this little town. Besides, I'm smarter than most desperate women. I wouldn't just open up to anyone, especially some creepy group of people."

"Well, that's another reason you could be in danger. The ones they find to have no value, they end up dead. Peggy, these people are dangerous. It's how I got the wound on my side! We were attacked by these people."

"Then you need to CALL THE POLICE!"

"Peggy...we are here to warn you. To try and give you a fighting chance. But we also really could use the help. Those children are still out there, and I can't do it by myself. That's why Gerard has agreed to help. The police, the chief... they are in the group. We can't trust anyone in the station."

"That's the not the only reason I'm helping the detective either, he..." Cutting him off before he tells her too much all at once.

"He's helping because we have become decent friends since he has spoken out as a witness to the abductions of Austin Douglas." Gerard gave me a look as if he is frustrated, I'm not telling her the whole truth. But I know that if we did all at once, it would either scare her away or make her believe we need to be in the loony bin.

"Okay, well what do I do, Detective? If you really think I'm in danger, what am I supposed to do different. You said you needed help, what can I do to really help you? Also, what is Moloch?"

"This is the part that gets a little hard to understand, you might think we are nuts. Moloch is a demon, and he has been manipulating the Disciples into handing over their children in exchange for the wealth or well-being that is currently absent in their life." Peggy Strout was a woman in her thirties that is currently wearing a tight pair of khakis with a yellow woman's polo; her name tag on the left side of her chest read (PEGGY) right under the Jenny's on top of the tag. She was a brunette, that wore dark thick framed glasses, and had some mid-life acne. She stood there after hearing what I had to say, doing her best to hold a stern look of invulnerability. trying to prove that she couldn't be fooled into believing anything.

I looked up from my coffee and met her gaze, with a wholesome look I told her, "It's all true."

"Listen guys, Moloch sounds like some dumb, boss from an old videogame. I'm *so* scared, *please don't take me Moloch*." Her voice filled with facetiousness, and mockery.

It was in that instant that the truck driver, the old mechanic labeled "Jake," and the elderly couple all were standing up looking dead at us. Their eyes filled with black and their stares full of morbidity. My body shifts and so does Gerard's. Scrambling to our feet, and Peggy attempting to see what's wrong. Looking at the old mechanic, "Jake, are you feeling alright, hun?"

As we got to our feet, the old mechanic leaped towards Peggy in a pouncing manor, like the decrepitly old man that had been ridden of his age and given the abilities of a wild animal. As he leapt, Gerard had grabbed and thrown the napkin dispenser, hitting him in the head. It temporarily knocked him unsteady, and in that split second Gerard grabbed Peggy's arm and ran for the door.

I reached for my gun and for the first time having the clip in it, fired at the man. He didn't move, but as the shot was fired off the others in the diner came rushing towards me, letting out the most eerie of caterwauls possible, making the hackles on my neck stand straight up. I, then, quickly turned and ran for the exit. Gerard and Peggy broke free of the horde-like situation by running out the door and getting into the car. As I reach the outside, and got closer to the car, I heard the glass on the door shatter as it had been thrown open. The men and woman were running now at an unreal rate, gaining on my tail. It was then Gerard popped the top half of his body out of the window. Sitting on the seal, and aiming down the iron sights of his rifle, letting off a large CRACK of a shot. It hit one as I heard the cries of pain, but I didn't care. These people have been taken, or possessed, by the demon Moloch.

I get to the car now, locking the door behind me. I jam the keys into the ignition and throw it into gear. Causing the tires to smoke as I peel out of the stationary position the car was in. The soulless bodies leaping onto the car, one on top and one on the windshield. The one on top slamming their fist onto the metal, as the other was pounding their head against the windshield causing cracks. With each hit of the head, the windshield cracked a bit more. His head splitting farther and farther with each hit, leaving more blood on the cracked point.

We were speeding up, steadily gaining five miles per hour by the second. It was then I reached around forty on the speedometer and slammed on the breaks. Peggy slammed forward, as she didn't have a belt on. But the possessed people on top of the car were flung forward and onto the pavement. At that moment I made the split decision to accelerate again, running over them with a loud THUD. We kept driving, and Gerard kept watch out the rear.

"We need a plan, and we need one quick." Peggy was now filled with an understandable amount of hysteria. She couldn't say much, but I could notice her trembling where she sat. Tears forming in the corners of her eyes, desperately wishing this all wasn't reality.

"WHAT THE HELL HAPPENED TO THEM!" Gerard looked at her for a moment and looked back out the rear window; he said subtly, "That's what Moloch does, and has done in front of us now twice."

"HOW ARE WE SUPPOSED TO STOP SOMETHING THAT CAN DO THAT!"

I understood where she was coming from, feeling helpless and scared. I understood that it wouldn't be easy trying to get over the fact we were just almost killed by possessed diner folk. To instantly feel alone in the world, and that everything has been turned upside down. This was my new reality, and unfortunately this was theirs. But that reality was about to get even worse because what lied ahead on the road was something far worse.

A roadblock from the Danville Police department and standing in the middle of the road was none other than Chief Smith.

CHAPTER 19

The line of police ahead was six cars deep, and seven officers, including Chief Smith. As we were closing the distance between us, I saw one of the officers extend the spike strips out. We had no choice but to stop.

"Detective, are you sure we should be stopping? I don't like how they are just sitting here waiting after what just happened at the diner."

Looking at both sides of the road, suppressed by the guard rails on both sides we didn't have any other choice. We couldn't make it over the sides, condemning us to whatever Hell the Chief and Danville police had in store for us. I started slowing down now, trying to conjure up a plan to get out of this alive. Gerard looked at me with fear and frustration in his eyes. Peggy was shaking and fighting back the tears of the remnants of the last fifteen minutes.

"Detective Hodge, turn off the vehicle and step out of the car." The Chief had a certain cockiness in his tone. He began to make the hand motion of turning the keys in the ignition, trying to tell me to turn the car off once more. I turned the vehicle off and had my hand on the pistol in my side holster. Gerard put a hand on my shoulder and grabbed my attention. While looking at him, he nodded his head as if he was reassuring me it's going to be alright.

I open the door to the car and stepped out. I started moving forward towards the chief and the officers. "Chief, something is going on here. I've uncovered a lot, and I have reason to believe there is a cult working at large."

"Detective Hodge, you and I both know it's more than that. You have a higher purpose, and I need you to come with me."

"What do you mean a higher purpose? Seems to me you are just trying to cover up whatever tracks you can, so you guys can keep doing what you're doing!"

"Detective, I assure you that whatever idea you have of this is wrong. Why don't you come with me, and let me show you?"

Looking back at Gerard, I can see that he is loading his rifle below the dash, just out of the officer's line of site. He was getting ready for whatever is needing to be done. But, seven on two is going to be a suicide. We need a better plan; I need to surrender myself. But, if I let them take me, then Gerard and Peggy will be left here with the officers which will most certainly get them killed.

"Detective, you need to come with me and fulfill your purpose." His eyes getting wider as he spoke, and a vein on his head becoming more exposed. "COME WITH ME NOW! COME SERVE YOUR PURPOSE! COME WITH ME! COME WITH ME! COME WITH ME!" With each scream, he is got more of a whining tone, and no longer forming words. Chief's eyes began turning black as night, and mouth elongating in length. Belting out a direful scream so deep an ominous that my skin began to crawl. BANG! Gerard had taken a shot and hit Chief through his neck, causing him to stumble a bit and gasp for air. It was in that moment I drew my pistol and began to aim for the officers closely behind as they started to draw their weapons. Noticing they weren't aiming in my direction; they were all focusing the car.

Aiming down the iron sites at the head of one officer I took the shot, dropping him instantly where he stood. Then quickly going down the line, hitting a second and a third. The next officer got a shot off towards the vehicle, and then another loud BANG has come from the car where Gerard had taken another shot. Dropping another one of them. I took another shot, and then another. Hitting each officer with a sense of precision that took me by surprise. By the last bullet, the officers were laying on the ground motionless, and bleeding out from the wounds.

I turn to look at Gerard and saw something was wrong. Peggy had been shot. I ran back to the car and open the backdoor to the cruiser. I see the blood covering the backseat, and that she had been shot in the chest. Holstering my gun, I take her shirt in both hands and began to rip it down the front. "Peggy I'm going to look at the wound." I see it and its entirety, having an entry point on the left side of the chest. She was struggling trying to get her words out, gargling on the blood coming up her throat now.

"Peggy, it's going to be okay. It doesn't look that bad. The detective and I will get you fixed up." Gerard was fighting back tears, and hands shaking bad enough he couldn't keep from dropping the fishing line he had brought from the cabin. Looking at me he asked, "Can we get the bullet out?"

As he looked at me, I notice the Chief standing behind him and grabbed him by the leg. Dragging him out of the car, and head bouncing on the pavement as he slid out of the car.

Standing in an upright position now, I redraw my pistol from my holster, pointing it at the Chief. The Chief looked at me and let out an utter shrill. I aimed the pistol at his head and pulled the trigger. The bullet perforating his face, just to the right of his nose and breaking into the sinuses, vacating the space once being used to influence his tone of voice.

"Are you alright, Gerard?"

He looked over at me and gave me a nod. But then looking back into the car, we saw Peggy lying motionless and eyes left open and in the last position she had left them. "Peggy! Say something to me! Peggy!"

I reach down with my index, and middle finger to touch the side of her neck. I felt no pulse. Peggy was dead. Yet another life taken by the infestation of darkness that dwelled in this town. Gerard holding his face in his hands and letting out a loud yell of frustration. It was then he got up and swaddled her body in his arms and started walking her over to an officer's vehicle. Opening the door and laying her in the backseat and closing the door.

"Gather the pistols and ammunition from the officers and put it in our car. I won't let her be taken over by that demon. WE OWE THAT TO HER, TRAVIS!"

I rather not say anything, but just agree and dispose of the bodies so they couldn't be used against us. I began taking out all the pistols and taking their mags. I put the ammo in the car and went back to help drag the bodies into the cars. Closing the last door, I see Gerard rip a part of his shirt into a few different pieces. Opening the lids to the gas tanks and shoving in the parts of ripped shirt he had. He took out the matches he had in his pocket from earlier, and the lit the cloth dangling out of the vehicle's tanks. On the way back to the car, I moved the spike strips out of the way so we can keep going.

Getting back in the car now, I put it into gear. Whipping the car around and started to head back in the opposite direction. Watching in the rearview I could see the cars one by one beginning to catch fire in an explosion.

"Detective, I don't want to drag any more people into this, we didn't help Peggy, we got her killed. Whatever it is we need to do, we need to do it on our own." I look over at him, seeing the tears forming in his eyes. And I start to feel the guilt and despair that overtook him. He was right, it was our fault that she had been killed. It was my fault. This whole situation is because of Moloch trying to get his hands on me. But what could have we done differently? All those people in the diner would have been possessed whether we would have been there or not. She would have been in that diner alone with all those people, where she would have been torn limb from limb. But knowing that didn't change the feeling I had. It didn't take away any guilt or pain.

I take out my phone and give it to Gerard. "Look up Moloch and see what you can find. Anything; legends, and or religious history. We need to know if there is anything we can use to our advantage."

Gerard's face changed with each page he is clicking on, from scared to curious to a loss of all hope. Meanwhile I'm driving aimlessly down the highway. I see the diner in the distance, meaning we are about to come up on the bodies I ran over earlier. "Keep sharp Gerard, we are about to pass the bodies we left in the road. We didn't burn them, so there's a chance they will be waiting for us."

Both of us looking so intently out each side of the car as we are driving. Hoping that we don't run back into the dark infestation of what used to be townspeople. Although I could see the bloody spot on the road where we had run the bodies over, they were no longer anywhere in sight.

"They aren't there, Detective; those things could be after us again before we know it!"

"I understand that… just keep looking for information on my phone."

Going back to looking at the screen he's mumbling under his breath. I didn't catch much other than the word "pointless." And I get it, it probably was pointless. But if that vision, or whatever it was earlier is true. I couldn't live with myself if I let those children stay that way and face that early death.

"I found something. Apparently, Moloch is from back in the Bible times. Kings and queens would take their children as sacrifices for riches and good fortune. The name MOLOCH means *KING*." Other than that, Gerard hadn't found really anything. Multiple websites had been checked, and he read multiples sections of online religious history in false gods, and deities. But nothing was to be found of a weakness, or a way out of this awful nightmare.

"I'm not seeing anything that would be any help to us right now. The only thing I can say is that it seems he needs the children to survive. WAIT! There are some old documents from Pagan history speaking of a Moloch.

Apparently, there was a deal made with the father of the underworld, as they call him, that Moloch will remain with power if he has children sacrificed in his name. He would be given the power of manipulation. Where he would be able to take advantage of young couples of an area swallowed by poverty and sickness. Promising them prosperity and comfort for the unspeakable price of their first-born son. Once the child has been born and was already promised to Moloch, a mark would appear. They call it the (Mark of the Reaping)."

"Gerard, we had a good idea about most of that already. Is there anything useful that we can use against him?"

"I was getting to that part. Once the Mark of the Reaping has appeared on a child, if he was to ever die before he was sacrificed to him..." Gerard looked at the phone with an unsettling gaze.

"What, Gerard? What would happen?"

"It says if they were to die before sacrificed, Moloch would lose the power of his domain and be drug back to Hell by something called (The Tormented)."

I wasn't sure how to respond. The way to stopping this awful creature was meaning death for...me. I couldn't let the children die, but the thought of having to take my own life was unbearable. But even with one of us dead before the sacrifice, the cult will take care of the rest. Keeping the name of Moloch living on. So, now I need to figure out somehow to make it all work. How will I save the children and get them to safety, and how will I die?

CHAPTER 20

I couldn't help but to think about the possibilities of myself dying before I came to Danville. How easy it would have been to have had an accident, and how many children's lives it would have saved. I couldn't help but to think of myself as an anchor for a malevolent demon. An anchor that as it drags the floor of the sea of children in this area, it decimates all in the surrounding path.

Just how many people have died because I have lived. I understand that could be said about any one of the children with this Mark of the Reaping, but that doesn't make me feel any better. But I can't help but wonder if my parents ever knew of this little detail. If they decided to keep me alive, rather than stop the cycle because they couldn't bring themselves to do it.

So many questions, and I didn't have the time to think about it all. I had to start making moves or we would lose the children.

We were coming up on the road that leads to the back side of the Morgan property. The road which seemed to be the boundary for where I started hearing the voice of Moloch in my head.

"Gerard, this is the road that will lead us to the children. Are you ready for this?" He nodded with fear in his eyes, but that fear was being forced out by rage and vengeance. Moloch had taken away someone who didn't deserve it, especially in Gerard's eyes. The situation had become real for him, after having to escape those backwoods brothers. But it became personal when they took the life of Peggy Strout. They weren't close by any means necessary, but to Gerard she was like him. Never really had love, never had kids, and was alone. I also assume that being from the same church gave him a feeling of relation. But with those connections in his mind, she was worth avenging.

I made the turn. The turn that would lead us to an unknown outcome. But also, the turn in which we might be able to save the kids. Driving along the road, I start getting an overwhelming sensation in my chest. Pressure built up, and then migrated to my head. I started getting a sense of spots in front of my face. My palms began to sweat, and my temples began to pulse. It was then I wasn't in my car anymore, I was in the Morgan's Manor. I see Corbitt Jenkins standing in the background and Mr. Morgan standing over Mrs. Morgan.

"HOW USELESS CAN YOU BE?! HOW IS IT POSSIBLE THAT YOU COULD DISOBEY WHAT WE HAVE BEEN TOLD TO DO? DON'T YOU REALIZE HE HAS GIVEN US EVERYTHING IN RETURN FOR MY SERVICE, AND OUR PATHETIC EXCUSE FOR A SON! YOU'RE A WORTHLESS, SIMPLE, PIECE OF BACKWOODS TRASH. I SHOULD HAVE LEFT YOU IN THE MUDDY DITCH OF POVERTY YOUR WORTHLESS PARENTS DUG FOR YOU!" He then gave her multiple blows to the stomach from his foot, and then grabbed her hair and started to drag her outside.

Corbitt, had been standing in the corner waiting for instructions. Nothing which he just saw fazed him, which shows it wasn't the first time he saw it. "YOU THOUGHT I WOULDN'T FIND OUT THAT YOU WERE TRYING TO HELP THAT WEEZLY LITTLE DETECTIVE? HE BELONGS TO MOLOCH; A DEAL WAS MADE BY YOUR SO CALLED 'BEST FRIEND'S' HUSBAND." Mr. Morgan dropped her in the back lawn, pinning her to the ground by driving his knee into her chest. He leaned over and whispered to her. "The best part about all of this is, you wanted to help your friend's son as some favor, when you were the one who helped me get in contact with them both. If it wasn't for you, she and her husband might still be alive."

Finding the strength to prop herself up in the grass, and blood coming from her mouth and nose. Mrs. Morgan was able to say, "The love and respect I have for Gracie-Anne is strong. Unlike yours which came from manipulation and fear. You took advantage of a girl in high school that had nothing and promised the world. You just didn't mention that it would cost the souls of hundreds."

As Mrs. Morgan was attempting to finish her sentence, Mr. Morgan began raising his foot and bringing it down on her head. Over and over, he had let her feel the full weight of his anger and frustration. Each stomp hitting a new spot on her head. Slowly coming from beneath her was a small pool of blood, and her teeth began to trickle into the grass next to her.

I could hardly understand how this woman was so dedicated to her friendship with my mother. Pretending to love this kind of man, would be insufferable. Hiding behind an empty smile, for what probably seemed to be an eternity. But when I saw them together coming in from a party for his firm, they seemed to be laughing and having a great time. But I guess that could have been influenced by the alcohol served at the banquet.

Corbitt then walked over and handed Mr. Morgan a towel for his shoes. He grabbed it from him and began wiping his shoes off. Corbitt then grabbed Mrs. Morgan and drug her off into the stable. It was then I was back in my car, and Gerard was yelling, and grabbing the wheel. "YOU'RE GOING OFF THE ROAD!" I immediately jerked the wheel back over to our lane and kept driving.

"Detective, where did you go? It was like you were gone for a minute. Are you okay?"

"I saw something else."

"Was it the children? Are they okay? Did you see little Austin?" Referring to his neighbor that he had grown fond of, Austin Douglas.

"No, it was Mrs. Morgan. She has been killed by her husband. A brutal death in their backyard. She was yelled at, demeaned, and her head stomped in."

Gerard was silent for a moment. Looking over at me, and just slowly shaking his head. "Well, we still have a chance of reaching the children. Whatever we need to do, Detective." I gave him a slight nod in understanding. We kept driving, and it was then I realized I had the map Mrs. Morgan had drawn for me to find the stable. I reached into my pocket and found the piece of paper and pulled it out. "Gerard, take a look at this and tell me what you see. We need to use it to find the stables where they are being held at." The map as he unfolded it, seemed as if it were drawn in a hurry. It was all in black ink, and the words written so fast on the map it appeared as chicken scratch.

"Alright, it says to take the highway we are on right now, and we should start seeing a small forest of pine tree on the right side." Not long after him saying so, we see the pines towering over us next to the road. They were all so tall and had dark green leaves from every branch. The farther we got, the more ominous it started to feel.

"Now, we should slow down because we will be coming up on a gate in a fence line." We kept driving and sure enough about a half mile down the road we find the fence line. Shortly after finding an old cattle gate. We pull into the small outlet in front of the gate. The gate an old silver color, with rust patches over the individual bars of it. A chain was wrapped around one end and a post right next to it. A padlock was holding it together, whether it was to keep people out, or keep people in. I got out and walked over to the gate. I started to jiggle the lock, and found it to be looking locked, but not fully connected. It was left in the position where it appeared to be. Mrs. Morgan had probably unlocked it for me, with the hope of me making it this far.

I pushed the gate open wide so I could get the car in and close it back. I hopped back in the car and pulled it through the gate. I parked it in a large group of trees and covered it with branches I found on the ground next to it. I reached over and opened the glovebox and grabbed a box of ammunition and grabbed my pistol from the holster. I started putting bullets in one by one starting to reload what little bullets I had used in the clip. Sliding the clip back in with a click, I put it back into my holster.

I got out and went back over to the gate where we came in. I started thinking about if we needed to get out with a fast escape, I needed to be able to ram through the gate. So, I took the chain and wrapped it loosely around one end and left the lock through one single link. I turned back around and started back for the car, and when I did, I didn't see Gerard.

"Gerard?" Trying to keep my voice low enough where no one would hear us. "Gerard, where are you?" It was in that moment I had a sharp pain in the side of my neck. I started feeling dizzy, and colors started flying in front of me. Fighting it as much as possible, I couldn't keep my eyes open. The only thing that pops up in my mind at this moment, is that I've been drugged.

CHAPTER 21

The sound of chains encountering other chains fills the dead room. The light, slowly pouring through the cracks of the old, and what seems to be, dry rotted boards making up the walls of this place. Struggling to gather myself, breathing shallowly. It is as if someone is pulling the threads of my consciousness, and preventing what I so desperately wanted to be, awake. Suddenly, I hear a door being opened, like someone had pulled back on a large metal latch. Shaking and breathing a little more heavily, I could not help but notice the smell coming from this place. It smelled of old dust, copper, almost like if you had a penny in your mouth and could smell a taste. Just as I was finishing my thought, I saw a figure coming from around the corner. A tall and dark figure, bellowing over what a normal sized human could naturally be. Where the Hell am I?

I was pulling myself together a little bit more by the minute. It was the sunrise, somehow Gerard and I had survived the night. But whether that made a difference, I didn't know.

I began to look around, noticing small details of where I'm at. It had an open feel to the inside, with small stalls along the walls of one end. Each stall had a four-foot door, with a cross board diagonally through the middle. It looks to be made to hold in the horses for an equestrian hobby or lifestyle. On the inside of the stalls were water troths, and a hanging hay troth.

But in the back of this large room was a more open space. It was occupied by a large work bench and hanging tools. The bench was covered stained red and started giving me the feeling of the backwoods brother's home. It was then I notice the figure coming back through the door and standing in front of the workbench. Observing closer, this dark figure looked to have horns making their way out of the hood covering his head. It was then I was sure, it was Moloch.

Watching his every move and waiting for him to come near me. His dark eyes and mine had locked gazes in that moment. He smirked and said, "Did you really think that you had a chance?"

He started walking away, and in the split-second small children appeared in front of me. Black peeling skin, looking to be burned, and eyes vacant from where they should be. These children were young boys and had an eerie way of movement about them. With each step their bodies jittered and moved unnaturally. It was then I felt a sharp pain again in my neck. I knew I just had been drugged again, and in response I turned around immediately. Finding a little boy looking down at me, when he saw that I had met his gaze he leaned over and his mouth stretched open, far past a regular child, and he screamed a high pitch scream.

Fighting to hold onto whatever consciousness I had left, I eventually started to doze off. The weight of my eye lids became too much to bear, and the state of insensibility was taking over.

***

A man's screams were beginning to rattle through the stable. Desperately trying to open my eyes, but quickly realizing they were weighed down by the remnants of the drugs injected into me. Focusing with every fiber in my soul to open my eyes. "OPEN!" It was in that moment I had opened them and saw the horror that they were shielding me from. Gerard was being dragged my multiple men and women into the large opening of the stable. They were all in dark red robes They looked at each other while standing all around him. Chanting had started, "Oblationem Et Da Pacem, Oblationem Et Da Pacem!" Completely in unison, and as the last word left their mouths, it went silent, they dropped to their knees and head bowed between their hands. The room was silent, not a single noise.

I'm trying to let out a scream, anything; to give Gerard a distraction to try and escape. But it didn't matter, I saw the children from before, only now there were eight of them. Skin scorched and black craters where they eyes had once been. They were creeping their way up to Gerard, and as they closed in on him, I could see them drawing blades. Each child had raised their blade and started piercing them into the abdomen and chest of Mr. Glover. The children were laughing, slowing turning from a laughter into cackling, and morphing into a high pitch shriek. Continuously impaling the man that had come forward to try and help with an investigation, the one witness. Gerard Glover, the man who was taken to his own slaughter like a pig, and after being saved giving gratitude by accompanying me on this God-awful trail of despair. From being saved, to still ending up with the same gruesome fate. I *was* alone before, and now even more so. Gerard's abdomen was torn open with multiple stab wounds. His ribs had been exposed and the blood had overtaken the floor-space underneath him. His eyes remained open, and his body laid cold and still.

    I was left in tears; Gerard had not only help me get here, he showed me a place when we needed to rest, he stitched my wounds after being stabbed at the house of those backwoods' maniacs, and he was a selfless man, that came into the station thinking he was doing right and reporting what he saw the night Austin Douglas was abducted. Not knowing that would end up being the start of his own death. To be abducted from his own home, forced into the back of a truck, and brought to a rotten flesh and stench filled basement. Where he was to be tortured and killed by those brothers. Gerard Glover deserved more than a chance at a real family in his life, he deserved more than someone like me.

    I gathered the strength to try and bring myself to my feet. Slowly rising and trying to not be noticed. Those children had finally stopped screaming, and the room fell to a hush. Staying perfectly still and trying to look through the crack of the stall door. The group of men in dark red robes were getting to their feet and grabbing the carcass of the man I had come to know. They were taking him out of the stable doors, and the children stood and began walking the opposite direction. The children began walking towards the walls of the building, the structure of the stable not stopping them as they walked straight through wall. I stood to my feet as I was the only one left in the room. And when I did, I saw that my leg had been shackled to the stall. The metal of the chain looking old, and aged. It was a darker black and grey color with small spots of rust forming along the link.

I started pulling at the chain, trying to break it loose from the large D-ring attached to the wood of the stall. But to no surprise I couldn't simply with my own strength. There had to be something I could use but looking around on the stall floor there was nothing but dust. Looking at the walls around me, trying to find any loose nail or anything I could get my hands. But it was no use. There wasn't anything close enough to me that I could use. Desperately pulling and tugging against the shackle, knowing that it wasn't going to make much of a difference.

Sometime had gone by and I could see that it was becoming late afternoon. The dust rising in the air, visibly showing through the small rays of light, breaking through the cracks of the walls. Starting to look up to the ceiling, knowing that at any time those people would come and get me. Showing me that same fate that was given to Gerard. Only with me, it would be in the name of Moloch, I would be burned alive. The thought of the heat pulling all the oxygen from lungs and suffocating me while scorching my skin was horrifying. But right now, I can't think of anything else to do but accept the fate I've had since the day I was born. Hope was not something I could find in this kind of moment, not even an ounce. But it was then I noticed while looking up at the ceiling I wasn't alone. Out of my peripheral vision I see a face staring at me. Turning my eyes in the direction of where I saw it, nothing was there. I bring my focus back to the front of me, and that's when I was staring face to face with one of the children that had killed Gerard. His eyes were not of Moloch, but black crater like holes. Skin dark and looking closer I could see the scorch marks from a fire. Slowly backing up a bit, that's when I notice this little boy, or what was left of him, was Charlie Mitchell. I could see his photo given to us by his parents, it was the first one I saw. But he had already been taken two months before I had been assigned to this case.

"Charlie? Charlie Mitchell? What happened to you?" The small child didn't know what to make of that. His head tilted sideways. Like you would see form a puppy trying to understand what "sit" meant. "Charlie, I'm so sorry this has happened to you. I'm in the same situation, my parents have sworn me to him as well." The boy started moving closer to me, and as he began to open his mouth a small, and tortured sound came from it.

"It burns…he burns… we all burn…" The words coming from him sending a chill up my spine. "Burn… Burn…BURN…" His voice slowly raising with each word. "BURN. BURN. BURN." In that instant the boy was gone, right before my eyes he had vanished. I frantically looked around, trying to see where he had gone. Then suddenly in my ear was whispered, "You'll burn too…"

I turned quickly to find no one there. I started tugging on the chain and shackle keeping me in this place. Desperately trying to escape, but there wasn't anything I could do. It was pointless, I've been chained here like a cow waiting for slaughter.

Suddenly I hear the door started to creek open, I duck down behind the stall and started looking through the cracks of the wood. Looking all around, that's when I see Corbitt Jenkins coming through the door to the stable. He was looking around and started to whisper. "Detective?"

He made his way over to the area I was in, and when he got closer, I raised from behind stall wall and said, "Back up!"

"Detective, keep your voice down. You'll get the attention of everyone here."

"What do you want from me, I know what Mr. Morgan has done! I saw you did nothing!"

"Detective, Mrs. Morgan had informed of what might happen. I was told to do nothing to raise suspicion of my loyalty to her husband, so I could try and help you. That was the Mrs.'s last wishes."

"What are you talking about? How you could you let Tim Morgan do that to her, his wife?!"

"Detective, she wanted to set things right. She wanted to try and help you. She has had the overwhelming guilt for helping him this far. Everything she did was driven from fear. But because of Mrs. Morgan's friendship with your mother, she couldn't live with her betrayal towards her and you."

"What are you saying Corbitt? That you are going to help me? What about the children?"

"Detective… All the children that were taken are dead. They have been for some time. You are the last piece to this whole thing. You are the last mark Moloch has been needing."

"What do you mean? Needing for what?" Corbitt Jenkins face had changed from remorse, to fearful. The look of unknown and horror had overwhelmed his expression.

"Detective, you are the last marked child needed for him to become full form, and part of this world permanently. Moloch has been bound to this small town and can't take his true form because of the lack of the last mark."

"Then why has he been taking more and more children? If I was all he needed, what was the purpose of the other children he has taken while I've been here?"

"Travis, the children that you were investigating have been dead for some time now. They were put to death the next day from the abductions. All of this was set up and made you to believe. Everything you've been told, everything you've seen. The news reporters that day in the station, the parents, they are all disciples of Moloch. Everything was made to make you believe there was some kind of ray of hope of saving these children. When in reality, they have been dead for days. This town has been damned for as long as I can remember. The fact that you made it out alive the first time was incredible. That's what Mrs. Morgan wanted me to make sure that you are able to do again. Leave this town, don't come back. Forget all of us here, and don't let Moloch have the last mark. If he takes his true form and goes from town to town. It will only be a matter of time until no one is safe from him."

Corbitt Jenkins pulling a key from his pocket and starting to unlock the shackle attached at my ankle. Rubbing where it had rubbed my ankle raw and looking at him. "What's going to happen to you?"

"You don't have to worry about me, I've dug my own grave. Its time I lie in it."

"No, there has to be something that can be done." Thinking of every possible outcome I could conjure up.

Nothing seems to sound possible. Fire is all that lies ahead of us both if I don't escape.

"That's it! Corbitt, where do they keep the fuel to ignite the sacrificial fires?"

"They keep them in the outer building closest to the Morgan Manor. Why?"

"Corbitt, instead of waiting to be found out, would you help me?"

"I don't see why I couldn't. If Mrs. Morgan wanted me to give you a fighting chance, my help is the best bet. What do you need from me?"

"I have an idea, but I'll need you help me keep watch. Can you get me to the outer building storing all the gasoline?"

"Well, it seems early enough we should be able to while everyone is preparing for the ceremony. Follow me."

Following Corbitt Jenkins out of the stables, I start looking around for any of Moloch's brainwashed slaves. I didn't see any now, but it could change with in an instant, we needed to hurry.

Rushing through the wooded area, to try and stay out of the open, we found ourselves near a building that looks like a large storage shed. Maybe for maintenance to keep all the tractors and equipment that keep up the land here. "This is it, Detective, inside you'll find all the cans of gas. What is your plan?"

"I'm playing it by ear, but is the building locked?"

"It shouldn't be, I'll go first and see if it's clear on the inside."

Watching Corbitt closely, he began to open the door and went inside. In a couple of minutes, he came back out and motioned to me to come in. I slipped my body through the small opening of the door and started looking around. Inside were two tractors, one green colored one with highlighted yellow trim, and then a red one. Next to the tractor was a four-wheeler and a side by side. All the things, I'm guessing were used to help maintain the property, and this was their maintenance and utility building. Besides the equipment, the only other thing I saw was the workbench at one end covered in tools. It smelled of new tires, and fuel. But I didn't see the fuel anywhere. "Where are the gas cans?"

"Right over there, Detective, they will be in front of the tractors. So, what do you plan on doing?"

"I'm going to try and make a trail of gasoline to the house and douse the inside with gas. Then once that's done, I need you to call out to the Disciples and have them come in for something. Once you get them all inside, slip out the back. That's where you'll find me blocking the exits and lighting the trail I might in the fuel."

"That's risky, what will you do about Mr. Morgan and Moloch?"

"Mr. Morgan you need to try and lure in there as well. As for Moloch, I'll be keeping his attention. You just make sure I get enough time to get the gas everywhere on the inside."

Corbitt Jenkins nodded his head and helped carry a couple of cans to the front of the house. As I was walking, I trailed behind the fuel so I could easily light it from a safe distance. Corbitt got to the door and called out to see if Mr. Morgan was on the inside. He didn't get any response, and that's when I ran in and started dumping the fuel over the curtains, and walls. I went especially into the study where it was almost like a library. I threw the gas up the walls, and all over the literature in there. Covering every square inch, I possible could. That's when I started taking the fuel upstairs and dousing the walls and stairs as I ran. Each room I spread the gas out over the floor and kept feeling an overwhelming feeling of hopelessness. But this seemed to be the best bet I had right now. Then I got to Chris's room. I couldn't help but to have tears start to fall. "I'm sorry, Chris… I'm sorry I was too late."

I began throwing the fuel everywhere over the room and running out. I got down to the bottom of the stairs and heard the door begin to open. I quickly got behind the corner and peaked around. Then Corbitt's head came around the door, and he whispered "Detective, come on! They are coming. I told them we were going to have some refreshments before the ceremony."

I grabbed the cans, ran out, and hid. I began watching the disciples load into the manor. Black robes with red stitching going in one by one. As soon as the last one stepped in, I grabbed whatever I could and started blocking the doors. I grabbed patio furniture and started piling it by the back door. After I had piled the last chair in front of the back door I had started heading towards the front when I suddenly noticed someone else coming from back behind the house, towards the field. I waited until the man had gotten close enough and started examining the patio furniture, and that's when I came out and grab him by the neck in a hold. He was squirming and fighting every second until his last. I dragged him to the front of the home and laid him up against the front door. I couldn't think of anything else to put in front of it anyway. As I looked at him propped up in front of the door, I started remembering having to burn the bodies of the men at Gerard's cabin. I couldn't stand the thought, so I turned away, and turned my brain off for the moment. That's when I ran back over to the outer building and thought to myself. How I'm supposed to light the fire?

I started looking around for something to start the fire. I went over to a small work area that had a couple of wrenches, and screwdrivers on the bench. I didn't see a lighter, or any matches anywhere. I went over to the tractors and started going through those. Still nothing, but it was in that moment I saw in the back of the side-by-side a box of cigarettes. It looked open, but not empty. I know that my old boss used to put the lighter inside the box to make it take up less space in his pocket. That's when I picked up the pack and opened it. On the inside was a chocolate brown lighter. "Yes!"

I brought back to the front of the building and went outside to light the path. I get close to the ground and try rolled the spark wheel. Repeatedly I try to get it to light, but nothing happens. So, I get as close to the gas as possible and make the sparks fly out towards the ground, just hoping one would catch. It was in that moment that one spark came out hitting the path, and the flame took off towards the manor.

The flame was speeding towards the home of Mr. and Mrs. Morgan, and as I was watching it, I saw the back door swing open and Corbitt was stepping out. I motion to him pointing towards the flame. In the split second he saw it, he took off running towards me and the building. When he made it about halfway was when the manor caught fire and went up in flames. Running at a faster pace he got over to me and we watched as the manor was engulfed by the flames.

The screams from the people inside, trapped and desperately trying to get out. A few minutes went by, and we started seeing people jumping through windows, on fire and rolling around in a last effort to try and suppress the flames.

At that moment the souls of the children Moloch had taken had appeared and started dancing around the burning bodies on the ground. They were singing "Ring around the burning, the people keep on turning, ashes, ashes they all will be dead. Ring around the burning, the people keep on turning, Ashes, ashes, they all will be dead." Hearing the singing had shaken me to the core.

It was then we saw more disciples coming over the hill from the fields. They were being led by Mr. Morgan. One of the disciples started yelling at the children singing in a circle. "STOP IT! STOP SINGING!" The children kept on singing in a circle, then the man took one of the children by the arm and tried yanking him out of the circle. In the split second it was attempted multiple boys jumped on the man and started thrusted the same blades they used on Gerard into him. The rest of the group kept clear of the children and started trying to help the others that were aflame. They group got closer to the manor and started doing everything they could to try and save the ones trapped inside. Mr. Morgan was standing in the back watching all of it happen. The expression on his face wasn't of concern, but anger and frustration. He began yelling, "HOW COULD THIS OF HAPPENED! In that moment I saw him direct his attention to the ones running by him to try and help the people set afire.

"You idiots, you are only going to get yourselves killed!" Looking at them, yelling trying to get them to stop. But it's like they were all drawn into that place on fire. That's when I saw Moloch starting to walk towards the flaming building where the people were.

Sun had just dropped below the horizon, and it began getting darker now. I couldn't help but notice Moloch's gaze on the people suffering, burning. The red and orange lighting flickering and reflecting off his black as night eyes. He started towards one of the disciples on the ground rolling around engulfed in flames. Moloch suddenly put a halt on the man's body by pressing his foot onto the man's chest. Making it impossible for him to roll and extinguish the flames on his body. Moloch held him down and watched as the man screamed for his life. Letting him suffer until he took his last breath. That's when he began to laugh and look up into the sky.

In a deep and spine shivering voice Moloch began to speak. "Burn... burn my disciples, burn for me. Burn for your savior!"

As soon as he said that he turned from the sky and began to look at Mr. Morgan. "Don't you want to show your tribute to me, Tim? Don't you want to show your loyalty?"

"Moloch... I've done everything you've asked of me. I've got all the parents to give you their first son. Why do I need to burn alive!"

"Do you think of yourself as significant now? Are you too good for you Savior?" Moloch began walking towards Mr. Morgan, and when he reached him, Mr. Morgan bowed and got to his knees. "I pledge myself to you Moloch, I'm devoted…," and before he could finish his statement Corbitt, and I watched Moloch pick up Mr. Morgan by the head.

"Moloch, my Savior… I beg of you to spare me! Have I not done great things for you? Deliver hundreds of children to you?" Moloch began to slowly lower him down to the ground, and as his feet met the grass, he drops to his feet and thanks him.

I started gasping for air, between the smoke of the manor, and the anxiety I could hardly breathe. Keeping my mind and trying to imagine slow breathing I finally start to get my breathing back at a normal pace. "Detective, what's our next step?"

But it was at that moment I turned to look at him, and one of the children of Moloch was standing directly behind Corbitt. Eyes vacant, still, and beginning to smile.

CHAPTER 22

I couldn't move, and Corbitt could tell by my face something was wrong. I looked to the boy, and I recognized the face. I could tell this was Austin Douglas. In a split second I say his name, "Austin?" Understanding his name, he shifted his focus to me for the time being.

"Austin, we need your help." His hands were thrown to his head, as if he was fighting an internal battle we will never comprehend. Moloch had to have been trying to maintain control, but Austin was fighting with all that was left of his being.

"Austin, I had help getting this far. Gerard Glover helped me get here, and he had his life taken trying to help save you all, to put an end to Moloch." As soon as he heard Gerard's name he lit up, looking to be triggering memories of his life spent here.

"Gerard told me how fond of you he was, he told me all the work you used to help him with. That you were close to him." Austin started letting out a slow growl, showing irritation with every movement he made. "You have to fight him Austin, you have to take back what's left of your mind."

He looked to me and whispered "Run, he's coming." It was then Corbitt, and I took off running. We started heading back to the woods where we came originally. Hurrying as fast as we can, we tried making it back to the car. I could see it in the distance, but it was in that moment the dark shadowy figure stepped out from behind a tree. Moloch, he had gotten ahead of us. The only thing we could do was make a sharp turn and start running in another direction. I yelled out to Corbitt, "Go left!"

We made a sharp turn and start running in the new direction. "CORBITT, IS THERE ANYWHERE WE CAN GO!"

"THERE IS AN OLD TOBACCO CURING BARN ON THE OTHER SIDE OF THE PROPERTY, WE CAN GO THERE!"

Running as fast as our legs could take us, I followed Corbitt. To our left I could see, coming up over a hill, people running full speed in our direction. It was who was left from the disciples that were burned in the fire. It looked to be six remaining people including Mr. Morgan. Options were running thin, and with it dark now, the cold kept worsening. With each step, and inhale of air a sharp pierce was jabbed at my lungs. The snow on the ground causing wet feet and deepening the chilling sensation in my body. It seemed hopeless, unrealistic, and impossible.

While running I kept an eye on the distance between us and the remaining disciples. Mr. Morgan leading them and wearing an expression of pure disgust. Corbitt surprisingly running at a good rate of speed and seeming to be doing fine.

In the distance in front of us, I could make out the shape of a large building. "Is that it!"

"Yes, if we can make it in there, maybe we can barricade the door." But even if we did manage to barricade the door. How much time would that buy us? What were we to do with some many people after us?

Getting to the door of the building, we get inside and immediately started piling things in front of the door. Old chairs, spare wood, and scrap metal we found. It appeared that this was no longer used for curing but for storage for junk. I began to look around for anything we could use as a weapon, especially since my pistol had been taken when I was drugged the first time. That's when I found an old branding iron, still looking to be solid. It was dark, and the only light we had were what rays we were getting through the cracks of the wood from the moon.

I see Corbitt pick up and old pitchfork, and now all we can do is try to come up with a way out of this. In that instant I turn and see a boy standing in front of me. The moonlight revealing his face just enough to recognize it was Austin again.

"Austin, we need your help, we need to be able to get out of this. Can you help?" The boy looked at me, and as he did, he turned and ran straight through the wall.

A few minutes had passed, and then Austin had returned. He held up his hand and gave me my pistol I had brought with me from the car. "Thank you, Austin!"

In that moment the pounding on the door started, and we could see it wouldn't last long. Then we hear from the other side of the door Mr. Morgan.

"Corbitt, how could you betray this family! After all we have done for you. You are just as guilty as we are for your cooperation in all of this!" Corbitt's face glowing from the small ray of moonlight and showing tears streaming down his cheek.

"Corbitt, don't listen to him. You told me that Mrs. Morgan's last wishes were for you to help me. This man murdered her in broad daylight! She was only trying to do the right thing and paid the price for it!" Corbitt Jenkins nodded his head at me and raised the pitchfork again.

The door becoming weaker and weaker with each hit it was taking. Bracing myself for them to come barging through the door, I start looking down the iron site of my pistol. The pile of junk began to move, and the door had been cracked open enough for a single body to make through.

Corbitt Jenkins charged for the first person to enter, a man I hadn't recognized at first, but then it was clear to me that it was one of the officers from the station. As soon as I could realize who it was, that's when the points of the pitchfork made contact with his chest. Piercing through and the sound of bones breaking filled the air. The officer began to cough, and that turned into a gargle the blood filling his lungs and throat. Struggling to breath, he let out a last cry for help. Wheezing from lacking the air, making the sound of his cry almost not existent, his head began to drop, and his whole upper half bent over the pitchfork as he fell dead. Corbitt jerked the pitchfork back, removing it from the man's body. As soon as he did the man collapsed to the ground.

The others started making their way through the small gap in the door. Aiming down the sight of my pistol, I put it to the head of the next person in, a woman. She was screaming and starting to throw herself at me. I took a breath and discharged the first round. It penetrated her forehead, and upon exiting the back of the skull, it left a trail of bone and brain matter to fall to the ground.

Seeing the face of the woman, as her body folded over itself reminded me of why I hated using the firearm. But in the moment my body was filled with adrenaline and fear, not leaving much room for remorse.

Corbitt was taking the pitchfork towards the door as another man was making his way in. Missing the man's chest as he was trying to squeeze his way through the door, Corbitt had half of the points through the right arm, and the other half through the neck. The man stops in his tracks, raising his left arm to his throat and struggling to breathe. Corbitt took the fork out of him and re-inserted it as fast as possible. This time fully through his neck. He was struggling to get it back out of the man, and while he was attempting to recall it back another man managed to squeeze through the door. He jumped on Corbitt's back and started to choke him from behind.

I quickly pointed the firearm towards the man choking him and took the shot. Clipping the back of the man's skull. He released Corbitt and dropped to the floor. But it wasn't long before the last three made their way in. Still having the gun, I pointed it towards the other men, including Mr. Morgan. But it was in that moment I had noticed something moving from the corner of my eye. I turned to see what it was, and when I did, I noticed a large, shadowed figure starting to stand to its feet. As it was rising the horns became more visible, and the face more recognizable.

Moloch stood there looking with his fiery orange and yellow tinted eyes. A slow, deep growl filling the room, and a hush fell over the disciples. He slowly started walking towards Corbitt. With each step followed a deep thud of his hooves. Frozen in fear, I couldn't bring myself to do or say anything. Then I looked over at Corbitt, filled with anger he began charging at Moloch with full force. Pitchfork directly in front of him and looking to find an end to this horrific nightmare. Moloch stepped to one side and grabbed Corbitt's arm and quickly squeezed. With the pressure from his grip, we all suddenly heard the crack of bone. The demon dropped him to the floor and shifted his glance over to Mr. Morgan. "Put an end to the problem you've caused for me... You will be the one to take this life." Mr. Morgan, with hesitation, slowly walked over to him. Moloch extending his arm out and handed him the pitchfork to finish the job. It was in that moment I knew I couldn't just let Corbitt die, not by the hands of the same man that brought this all upon this town. I drew my gun and aimed towards the man who started all of this. The disciples yelled out to him as I did, "MR. MORGAN, HE HAS A GUN!" He quickly looked in my direction, and in that split second right before I fired my pistol, I hear Moloch say, "That's it Travis... do it." The next thing I know, Mr. Morgan had a hole in the middle of his forehead. Looking at me wide-eyed and not able to speak. His body dropped forward and as he was falling the pitchfork had shifted in his hands, causing him to land right on the business end of it. Going through his neck and propping his upper body off the ground. It was almost as if he was one the bear rugs you would see in a hunter's trophy room. Mouth open, head propped up, while the rest of the body laid flat on the ground. Just like that, the man who had damned this town by taking a deal from this demon, was laying there lifeless.

Moloch walked over to where Corbitt was on the ground and bent over to grab him by the throat. He lifted him up to eye level and said, "For your insolence, and betrayal I bound your soul to fire and damnation." Immediately tightening his grip and snapping the neck of Corbitt Jenkins.

CHAPTER 23

Corbitt Jenkins, the man who served the Morgan's manor for years, loyal and caring member of their household, at least he was to Mrs. Morgan. As he was hanging there lifeless in the hands of Moloch, I began to wonder if there really was anything I could do. If all the lives that have been lost getting me this far were for nothing. Gerard Glover, Stephanie Morgan, Peggy Strout, and now Corbitt Jenkins. What if all of it was pointless, and Moloch would soon be set free into the world by taking true form.

Suddenly the children came from the walls and surround me. One coming forward and grabbing the pistol from me. As he was taking the gun, Moloch dropped Corbitt Jenkins body. As it hit the floor the sound of the carcass breaking even further made me jump. The demon raised his hands and said aloud, "Rise my children. Rise my Disciples!" The lifeless bodies lying on the ground began to move. Slowly one by one, they stood to their feet, and then Corbitt's body began to rise. Against his will, another soul taken and for some reason his made tears begin to fill my eyes.

"Corbitt, I'm so sorry…"

"Boy… I told you. It doesn't matter what you do, or where you hide. This is what was promised to me, and I will have what's rightfully mine. Get ready for the tribute and drag him back to the stables until things are ready."

The disciples, alive and dead, started restraining me. While I was being held down, others bound my hands by spare barbed wire that had been stored in this curing barn. The tighter the wire was wrapped the farther the barbs pierced into my wrists. As blood started to pour and roll down my hands, the only thing I could think was that this was it.

Two of the disciples stood me up and began forcing me towards the door. The others were clearing out the things we had barricaded it with and opened it for us to go through.

Cold was the night, and the moon scintillating. The light reflected off from the snow on the ground, giving it a slight purplish tint. The brisk breeze was tumbling over it and making a small trail of sparkling icy dust. The beauty around me wasn't fitting to the grim fate that I was marching towards.

I could see the smoke now that rising above the remnants of the Morgan manor we had burned. Walking up over the hill, I could see where it once stood. I could remember the first time driving up to it, so beautiful and misleading. Although the exterior was radiant with beauty and elegance, I never knew the history of how it came to be were so dark and morbid.

I couldn't help but to think of all the things in this malevolent place that had fooled me. The job that appeared online with such perfect timing, as I was itching for a promotion. The people in the station that I always had the feeling they were talking about me while I was walking out of a room. The simplistic lifestyle that I thought I could have while living here. But I couldn't have been farther from the truth. This place sucked me in and never intended on letting me inhabit it.

All these people, driven to such a level of desperation they were willing to follow or even worship a demon that came to be here. Moloch had fed off their desperation and had help from Tim Morgan to lure them all into this trap. What would come of all the people if I had never come along and burned the manor? Would they really have been able to live free lives? Or rather than followers, were they slaves to their situation and manipulation? But with that same notion I couldn't feel bad for anyone agreeing to the heinous thing they've all done.

We were coming up to the stable now, and I knew this would be the last stop I had before being sent to my execution. The disciples opened the door and forced me over into the stall where I was originally. They forced me to the ground and put the shackle back on my ankle. I was out of options and left with nothing but an aching heart of failure.

The disciples left the stable, and I could hear Mr. Morgan, or at least what used to be, instruct the others on how to set up the sacrificial ceremony. The details that were involved sounded precise, and all with reason.

"You three need to go and get the wood for the fire. You need to make sure the Tophet is ready for the sacrifice. The rest of you need to make sure you are ready for the ritual."

I started peering through the cracks of the stable. Looking at the stars I could see and remembering my foster parents letting me go on a camping trip with school when I was younger. We went to the Mark Twain National Forest and camped for two nights. We never used our tents, because when we went, the bugs were already starting to fade for the season. We camped in our sleeping bags right on the ground next to the fire and stared up at the stars. Not once did I ever feel like I had a chance to get onto the police force. But somehow, I overcame the fears I had, as well as the physical side of the testing. Things were so simple then; I knew nothing of where I came from or the evil lurking in the rearview of my life.

I had dreamed of one day finding someone who loved me, someone to share my life with. I planned on having children and being able to pick them up from school. To be there on the day of their weddings, and someday become a grandfather. I wanted my fantasized family to know who I was, to never doubt where they came from. I never wanted my children to have the feeling of unknown. Or to wonder whether they were loved or had someone always in their corner.

I always dreamed about saving lives. To solve cases whether they were big or small. To make a mark on this world and help. I remember feeling the joy I had when I had passed the police academy, the boost it gave my confidence. But still at the same time, denial that it happened. A boy that was raised in foster care his whole life, coming from nothing, and turning his life into something. It all just didn't seem real, until I showed up for the first day on duty. Having the uniform on and representing a badge. Having something that I earned, something to be proud of. That maybe my life finally had purpose. Up until then, I struggled with understanding how my life possibly could. If my biological parents didn't want me, if I wasn't good enough for them, then why would I be good enough for anything?

Then that dreadful night that Mrs. Morgan had met with me to try and help with what I thought was a case, but really my planned death. She wanted me to know that I had a mother that loved me, that wanted the best for me. But due to my father making a horrible mistake, that life she wanted for me was put into jeopardy. Mrs. Morgan gave me a piece of my life I had been missing this whole time, and it took up until this moment to really make me understand the full magnitude of her actions. She told me of the wonderful times that had growing up, something my mother should have been able to tell me herself. She explained the question that I had harbored all these years as to why my own parents could abandon me. I think I finally understand what she did, she didn't want to make sure I stop Moloch. She probably knew it was impossible. She wanted me to finally know how dear I was to my mother, her best friend, and that I truly was loved. Loved enough to make a horrific sacrifice of leaving a child in an unknown place to be cared for by complete strangers. Mrs. Morgan wanted my mother's love to finally reach me.

CHAPTER 24

It's probably been an hour or so since they chained me up in here. All this time just reminiscing on the past and all my aspirations. With all of it being encouraged by my soon to be demise, I still couldn't help but feel almost bliss. All this time, I've felt alone, and now understanding a bit more of what was done for me, I couldn't help but to be a little grateful for the love that's been shown.

Yes, it was started with a terrible mistake by my father. But that mistake was made in hopes to save my mother's life, which it did for the time being. Even though how terrible everything was, the deceit, the manipulation, I know that inside me I'm a little more complete for knowing the truth.

It was then I suddenly heard the door latch move, and the door started swinging open. It was a couple of the disciples to retrieve me for the sacrificial ceremony. Moloch's children started to appear from the walls around me as the disciples were unshackling me and escorting me out of the stable. Circling around us and singing in the toon of "Ring Around the Rosie." "You'll be one of us, you'll be one of us, burning, burning, your soul will be his."

Continuing to sing as we are leaving the stable, each verse becoming more and more off tune.

We kept walking, and I could start to hear the chanting of a crowd of in the distance. In front of us over the hill I could see the light from a fire burning bright enough it was lighting up the area around it. The chanting was getting louder the closer we came. It was loud enough the words began to be clear. It sounded familiar; it was the words they were chanting when Gerard was killed earlier. "Oblationem Et Da Pacem, Oblationem Et Da Pacem! Oblationem Et Da Pacem, Oblationem Et Da Pacem!"

Coming up over the hill, I see the disciples surrounding the Tophet they had been preparing. A statue in the shape of the Moloch symbol built and on fire, so large that you could feel a small amount of heat from where we were. Hot enough that most of the snow around the area had been melted, and dirt was visible. The Tophet was in front of that fire and was piled with sticks, clothes, as well as mounds of hay for kindling. Inside the Tophet was a large stone table awaiting the body they intended on being the sacrifice… me.

As we were approaching, I saw that there was a large chair, a throne, made of stone and reflecting the light from the fire. Walking around it now and taking a seat was Moloch. When he sat down, the souls of children he had kept started emerging from the darkness behind him. They were walking over to the table and started making a high pitch shrill that seemed to echo over the disciple's chanting. We had reached the edge of the circle of disciples. They made an opening, and I was thrown to the ground in front of the fire.

Moloch lifted his hand to hush the crowd of disciples, as when he did the only thing that could be heard was the roar of the fire. Still bound by the barb wire on my wrists, there was nothing left for me to do but accept the fate I was damned to.

Mr. Morgan stepped forward and began speaking to the Disciples of Moloch. "Brothers and sisters, we are here on a great occasion! We have gathered here to offer up this tribute to our savior Moloch!" The crowd roared with cheer and worship.

"We are offering this man right here!" Pointing his index finger directly at me. "We sacrifice this man in the name of Moloch. We sacrifice this man for the great honor of unbinding our savior from this place, to spread his kindness and power throughout the world!" When those words left Mr. Morgan's lips my skin began to crawl, and chest began to sink. I've failed, and this will be my end and Moloch's beginning. Moloch and his ghouls had killed Gerard, Corbitt, Peggy, Mrs. Morgan, and both of my parents. What chance do I have, what reason do I still need to live?

"This man was able to get away once with the help of his harlot of a mother, and disgrace of a dad! This man, marked by our savior Moloch, was promised to him by his own father and still survived all these years! Are we really going to allow that! That slander against our lord!" The other disciples raised my body up and pulled me towards the Tophet, getting ready to take me in to place me on the table.

Before they could, Moloch raised his hand and hushed the crowd of followers and began walking over to me. Now standing just a few feet away he said, "Bow to me!" It was then a felt a hard hit to the back of my legs, which made me drop to my knees. Moloch towered over me and looked at me with such hatred, and disgust. "It's time I own up to my promises. It's time you understand that you never had a chance of escaping me, MOLOCH. My power is too great, and I'm all seeing! I'm all knowing! Now you will be mine and do my bidding as I request for all eternity!" Moloch turned away from me and returned to his throne.

It was in that moment that I realized; Mr. Morgan was right. I had survived all this time, because of my mother. I was given the chance to live! How could I give up? How could I allow myself to be taken by such a thing as Moloch? I won't do it! I won't give him what he needs, I'll take my own life before he is given the chance to! Suddenly realizing I was still bound by barb wire and had no way of escaping.... Barbed wire! That's it!

I pointed my head to the sky and could only think of one thing. "Thank you, mom, for giving me the chance to live. But I won't allow this to happen to anyone else! I started rotating my wrists, and with each rotation the sharp edges of barbs began digging further and further into my wrists. The pain was so unbearable, but I can endure a little pain at the price of so many more children's lives.

The blood began to pour from my wrists, and I could see it starting to come around my knees on the ground. My head started feeling lite, and my wrists could no longer feel any pain. That's when I hear one of the disciples scream out, "He has slit his wrists with the barbed wire bindings!" Moloch stood up and let out a loud and deep yell. "NO! WHAT HAVE YOU DONE!" It was then I fell over into the dirt face first.

Turning my face to the side, I could see him throwing disciples in his way directly into the fire. Screaming as they caught fire, and the souls of the children laughing from amusement. The disciples by me trying to pry the barbed wire off my wrists, and as soon as I feel my wrists free, they dropped to my sides and that's when I saw it. The light from the moon had gone away, and the fire had been put out by an immense wind. The ground in front of me began to split open and shining from the crevice's mouth was a flame so hot it burned the skin on my face. As if I had just opened a pre-heated oven door and the heat had hit me. The surrounded snow instantly melted on the sides, and the melted snow ran off into it.

From the crevice in the Earth came crawling out terrifying looking beasts. Their claws so long, and hands so large. Their skin was a mixture of burning flesh soaked by the heat boils bursting and pouring over it, and scars from what appeared to be whips. Horns emerging from both sides of their skulls and curled almost in a complete circle. Suddenly I had remembered what Gerard had said. These horrifying demons…were The Tormented.

Dozens of them came crawling up from the crevasse splitting the Earth's surface, and all began grabbing Moloch.

It was then that one of them got right in the face of Moloch and said, "It's time you go with us… Don't worry, we are going to have so much fun with you…" As soon as it said that he opened his mouth to show a smile. Revealing a multitude of large sharp, and crooked teeth.

One by one they started grabbing different parts of Moloch's body, bringing him to his knees. Moloch let out a roar and began clawing that the ground around him as he fell to his stomach. Dragging his body closer and closer to the crevasse, and when they got close Mr. Morgan ran towards the Tormented and had flung himself at one of them and began yelling. "You won't take our savior!" Grabbing ahold of the Tormented and not letting go. The Tormented let out a shriek, and snatched Mr. Morgan from his body, and hurled him straight into the fiery pits from which they came.

Moloch began tearing away at the ground around, clawing desperately in the attempt of being set free. He grabbed one of the Tormented and ripped him off one of his sides and threw him back into the crevasse. As soon as it happened, the rest of the Tormented all sank their claws deep into him. Moloch let out a cry of agony, "THIS ISN'T OVER!"

My eyes then began to feel so heavy, and as I was about to close them, I watch the Tormented drag Moloch over the edge and back into the depths of Hell from which they came.

The ground closed where it had severed apart, and the flames were quenched. The light of the moon had taken back the presence over the Earth once again. The bodies that were once reanimated by the demon, Moloch, had started to drop to the ground. After he had been dragged away, I'm guessing the power he had over them disappeared as well. The three remaining disciples took off running in the direction of where the manor used to stand. The souls of the children that had been damned for an eternity slowly started to dissipate. But at that moment, my eye lids were so heavy, and my consciousness was starting to fade in and out,

I saw Austin standing a little bit in front of me. He raised his arm and began pointing. I look over in the direction in which he was pointing and saw someone walking towards me. It was then I started to fade, and my head fell to the ground.

***

Feeling a sharp pain from wrists and my eyelids heavy I slowly open them and bat my eyes. Blinking multiple times trying to adjust to the light coming in through the window next to my bed side. I began to look around and sitting in the chair next to me was a man in a light khaki colored overcoat, wearing a tie, and slacks. His thick black glasses pulled to the edge of his nose as he was reading a book. The man notices me moving and looks up. He pushes his glasses back closer to his eyes and says, "Oh, you're awake, that's great!" I couldn't help but to give him a peculiar look.

"Travis, my name is Robert Knoll." In that moment my brain flashed back to when Gerard and I were speaking about possible people that could help us, and when I went to search for this guy's name online nothing came up for him. So, we couldn't reach out for help.

"How do you know who I am?" Looking at him and waiting for his answer, my stomach let out an enormous growl.

"Well, it seems like you're hungry! Travis, I saw your name from your identification in your wallet. I looked when I got you here to the hospital in Lexington."

"Well then how did you know where I was when I needed help!"

"That's more complicated to get into. Why don't we just start off with how you are feeling?" I tried moving my body some and was overtaken by extreme fatigue. My arms barely had any strength left in them and chest heavy.

"I guess, I'm alright, all things considered. But how did I survive? How did I get here?" Robert looking out the window took in a deep breath. He turned his head to look at me and responded with, "When I got to the ritual site, so much had already happened. A couple, a man and a woman were fleeing the scene, and that's when I saw you lying on the ground. I noticed the large pool of blood gathering under your body, so that's when I cut the wire around your wrists and wrapped the wounds. I picked you up and carried you to my SUV and drove you straight here."

I couldn't believe that this was possible. I don't see how it could be. "But, how did you know I needed you? I need to know. This all doesn't make any sense!"

Robert looked at me and continued to set his book down. "Travis, I'm a demonologist. I have been sent to this area by the church a few months ago. There had been some reports of missing children, and that it had been going on for some time. The fact that higher authorities never came to assist with the cases, such as the Federal Bureau of Investigation, was a large sign that it was time, we stepped in. So, the church had sent word for me to come and investigate. I came and started creating a front for people to think I was building a life in Danville. I got a small place and started looking around town. I went to church, I started looking for work and I even started speaking to truck drivers that would stop in at a diner south of here to see what they had heard. But it wasn't until I overheard a conversation being had with a man by the name of Tim Morgan. He had sat down and started speaking with a new couple that had come to town and were struggling with bills. Mr. Morgan told them there was a way he could help them, and their troubles with money would no longer be an issue."

I couldn't say anything, the fact he started uncovering this on his own was more than impressive. But realistically I'm more thankful than anything.

"That's when I made an anonymous phone call to the police, I knew I was going to need help if they were being lured into a dangerous situation. But when I reached the station, my call was transferred to the Chief immediately and he started acting strange. Chief Smith started asking me about where I had heard the information and to please just come down to the station. Insisting that if I was going to make this kind of call, they would need to speak with me in person first, rather than wanting to save the lives of that young couple being swayed by Mr. Morgan. So, at that point I knew the best thing for me to do was follow breadcrumbs and see where I could get."

"How did you end up at the manor? How did you know where to look?"

"I didn't exactly know where to look, but I did know I needed to find the place where Tim Morgan was living and start there. I waited to see Mr. Morgan in town, it took a few days until I saw him again. Then a few nights ago I saw him stop at the gas station, dressed in a full suit. It looked as if he was coming from a party, and when his wife stepped out of the vehicle, I noticed they had been drinking. That's when I knew it would be the perfect opportunity to follow them, and see where it was, he lived."

"The party, for his firm. I was there on that night. Waiting for them to return, so I could question them about the disappearance of their son."

"Yes, and that's when I first saw you. I followed them home and saw the Morgan manor for the first time. I parked right outside of their drive and got out to look around a moment. When I did, that's when I saw you coming out of their drive. I waited a few more minutes and as soon as you were gone from sight, that's when I saw Mrs. Morgan come down the driveway and head in the same direction. I turned on my car and left the headlights off and followed her. When I saw her go into the police station, she was in their probably around fifteen minutes or so. When she came out, she ran to her car. After that, she went into a little convenience store, and when she came out, she had a cheap new phone she had just bought. She sat in her car for a little bit and took off again."

"She bought the phone to call me, that was the same night she met me to tell me the truth. About everything that had been going on, and about my parents." Looking around while he was talking, it was starting to all come together.

"I didn't see where she went after buying the phone, but as she was pulling out of the store's parking lot, I did see her on the new phone talking with someone. That's when I got out of my vehicle and went inside to get a coffee. As I was paying, I looked to the back of the store where the employees could count the drawers and things and saw a man on the phone. A call that he was trying to keep quiet. But that the last thing I could make out from reading his lips was, '*Thank you Mr. Morgan.*'"

That's how it happened, that's how Mr. Morgan was tipped off that she had been trying to help me. I couldn't bear the thought of what had happened to her for trying to tell me about my mother. About how I could help those children.

"After seeing that phone call happen, I immediately went back to the house I had been staying at and called my boss. I told them what I thought had been going on and told him about Tim Morgan. It was then he informed of his theory. He told me all about the demon that had called himself "King," or as they called him back in the days of Canaan, Moloch. He explained to me that Moloch's intentions were to become of this world, so he could wreak havoc upon Earth and be worshipped. But, in order to do that he would have to be able to have people sacrifice their sons to him willingly. I was told about "The Mark of the Reaping," and once a child has been marked, it can't be undone. After all that it wasn't until I saw the large fire lighting the sky that I started heading towards the Morgan property. But when I got there, it was already too late. That's when I found you."

"But, if I'm still alive, how was Moloch dragged back to the pits of Hell? I had to die before he was able to sacrifice me in his name. That was the only way to stop all of this! Wouldn't me living reverse things?"

"Satan is not omniscient; through the eyes of Moloch, he saw that you were on death's door. With how deep your wrists were lacerated, it's a miracle I got you here in time. With that Satan would have thought you were sure to die and forced Moloch back to where he came."

As soon as he said that I reached for my sleeve and began to push it up. As I was rolling the gown's sleeve up

Robert's eyes widened a bit. I could see him noticing the branded-like white mark on my arm. "My father swore me to Moloch in order to save my mother from cancer many years ago."

"How are you still alive? It doesn't make sense that you would have been spared."

"I wasn't spared, my mother snuck me out of Danville when I was an infant and left me in Indiana where I was raised in foster care my entire childhood. I never knew my parents."

Robert leaned over and put his mouth into his hands. Looking at me and the mark, I could tell he was intrigued.

"But you were fine growing up? How did you end up back in Danville?"

"A couple of years ago I became a police officer, and then a few weeks ago, I applied online for a position I had found. It was a promotion to detective status here in Danville. Mrs. Morgan had helped them find me, and when she did, they set the whole thing up to get me to come. As soon as I got here, they put me on this case to investigate the children's disappearances. Why they would do that I have no idea, but it wasn't long after terrible things began uncovering."

"It's possible that there is a range Moloch was able to sense you, but while you were out of Danville, he couldn't sense you at all. Interesting…"

"I'm not sure, all I know is that because of him looking for me, and trying to lure me in, some really good people were killed." Robert stood up and walked over to the window. While looking out of it he scratched the side of his face and turned to look at me.

"Travis, I know it's been a long road, and this experience was completely horrifying. But what do you see for your life now? What is it you're going to do with this second chance?" I looked at him for a moment, then turned away. I hadn't thought about if I lived through all of this, it never even crossed my mind. I really didn't know how to answer that, because I'm not sure I had the same motive as I did when moving to Danville.

"Robert, over the past few days…. I've seen awful things. I've had to do unmentionable things, and I've had to lose people that were only trying to do that right thing when helping me. I'm not sure what I should do anymore."

Robert stared at me for a few minutes, without saying anything. Then he came and put his hand on the side of the bed. Looking at me with the straightest of faces and said, "What if I told you we could really use your help? That working for the church, we could prevent things like this from happening to other children. That YOU could help save children all over the world, possessed by demons. What if I told you by coming with me, you could make an honest difference in this world?"

"Helping people and making a difference was all I've ever wanted. To save the lives of ones who couldn't save themselves. But, fighting off demons and the wicked like what I've had to deal with here, I'm not sure I'm cut out for this."

"Travis, if your survival wasn't a sign that you weren't meant to help with this fight, I don't know what is. Besides, Moloch was dragged back to the depths from where he came. But once it's known that the last Mark of the Reaping is still alive, don't you think you'd be better off with people on your side?"

When I heard those words, my heart sank. The thought of it shook me, but I was given this chance for a reason. My mother, Mrs. Morgan, Gerard, Peggy, and Corbitt all put their lives on the line to try and help me. I couldn't let all of that be in vain.

I looked up at Robert and nodded. "You're right, and when he does come back, I want to be ready. I want to prevent this from ever happening again."

"Do not be overcome by evil but overcome evil with good. My Lord is fighting the battles of the LORD, and evil will not be found in you all your days. That's from the book of Romans, and it gives me strength as I hope it can you. I can't promise you this will be an easy path, or that it will be a pretty one. But I believe our Father in Heaven has a plan for you yet."

It was hard taking all this in. Robert went on talking about his line of work. The insane cases that he has been assigned to, and some of the horrible things he's seen. But somehow it made me feel somewhat better that I wasn't alone in this world, that I wasn't alone in this. But even with that feeling it still didn't seem like it would be enough to stop him… I didn't even want to keep thinking his name, Moloch.

He read to me from the Bible, and I told him about how I had heard his name from Gerard. He was sad to hear that such a good man had passed but pleased that God had given him enough strength to over the fear in this situation. But even with all this talk, and the blessing of having a second chance. The thought of a God in heaven looking down over us, watching all this terror and misery happen still made me question his existence. Why would he let it happen being as awful as it was? Why would he spare my life, when clearly, I should have died in that field? Whatever the reason, I'm grateful. I just wish I knew what to believe in anymore.

It was starting to get dark now, and the doctor had just come in to tell me I should be released in the morning. Robert began telling me about where we would be going, and that I could send someone for my things. Apparently, we were going to be headed to St. Louis in eastern Missouri. I used to live not too far from there, but never went. I never had any reason to, other than a field trip I had missed going to the St. Louis Arch in the fourth grade. I had gotten the flu the day before we were supposed to go, so I didn't end up being able to.

As Robert was talking, I slowly started drifting off to sleep. I couldn't hold my eyes open any longer, the meds the staff had given me to rest were taking a toll on me quickly.

***

It was the next morning, and I was trying to keep my eyes open. Whatever the nurse had given me to help sleep, sure helped a lot more than Jameson ever had. It took me a few minutes to even get moving around. I had got dressed in clothes that were laid out for me. I'm guessing Robert had brought me some clothes to put on since mine were trashed. There was a pair of jeans, some of a darker color. A black shirt with the Guns and Roses logo on the front. As well as a dark green cargo jacket and boots. It looked as if he had just stopped in a Wal-Mart and grabbed me whatever he could find in my size. But I'm not complaining, what he got was pretty comfortable even with the injury and fatigue.

After getting ready, a nurse brought in some breakfast for me while I was waiting on being released by the doctor. I sat and ate while waiting on the word I could leave. At that moment Robert walked through the door.

"Great, the clothes fit. I just grabbed whatever I could find that would be suitable for the weather. It will be colder once we get farther north. How are you feeling?"

"Not too bad, still plenty of fatigue. But I'm sure it will pass quickly. Hey man, thanks for the clothes and all of this. You didn't have to do any of this."

"Well, now that you are wanting to help in our fight. You can count on me to have your back. But honestly, I would have helped you either way with all of this. After what you had been through, and I wasn't there fast enough. I can't help but to feel like I let you and many others down. All those children taken and burned. The countless people that have come to find out something and were killed to keep the secrecy of what had been going on. You were tricked into coming here and lured into all of this. I just wasn't quick enough, and I won't let that happen again."

As he was saying all of this to me, he grabbed some type of red necklace from his pocket and wrapped it around his hand. On the end sticking out of his fingers was a cross. He took his fingers and pointed to the head, then down to the stomach, then from one side of the chest to another. He then began to pray in a whisper liked volume. The remorse that he had, the passion in his line of work made me feel like this could be something worth dying for. Knowing that made going with him much easier.

As he finished praying, the doctor had walked in with a clipboard in one hand, and the other in medical coat pocket. "Alright, Mr. Hodge, you're free to go. But you need to rest a couple days, try, and take things easy. I gave him a subtle nod and started to put my coat on."

As we were walking out to Robert's SUV it started sinking in that after all of this, I could be okay. We continued walking down the hall and passed some of the staff that had cared for me. One of the nurses stopped me and said, "I'm so glad you're doing better Mr. Hodge. Just remember, there is always someone out there that cares very much for you." It wasn't until a few minutes later that I understood why she had said that to me. I came into a hospital with severe, life-threatening cuts on both wrists. She probably thought I had attempted suicide. With there being some truth in that, she will never know what I was willing to do that for.

We got to the front doors, and Robert said, "I'm parked right over here. Do you want me to pull up to the front or can you walk?"

"I'm fine, man, I can walk." So, we headed over to the vehicle. It was black and had on the rear the word "Expedition." In the center of the tailgate was the Ford symbol. I opened the passenger door and managed to pull myself up into the seat. I closed the door and put my seatbelt on. When he started the engine, I could feel seat beginning to warm up underneath me. I noticed on the dash he had turned the seat warmer on for me.

But suddenly the heat wasn't the only thing I was starting to feel. An enormous amount of pressure began to build in my chest. The pressure pushing up to my head, and the mark on my arm began to burn.

"What's wrong, Travis? Do I need to go get a nurse?"

I started seeing spots in front of my face, then it was like I was no longer in Robert's vehicle at all. It was dark, and I could barely see anything. I heard a deep and slow growl. I turn and see no one behind me. Then I heard the cries of a woman, desperate and in pain. "Travis…. Help me! My baby won't you help me!" Frantically trying to find the voice calling out to me.

"Mom! Is that you Mom!" But there was no reply. Just more agonizing screams. Then suddenly the screams had stopped, and the deep growl was back coming from behind me. I turn slowly to find looking right at me the eyes filled of fiery orange and yellow.

"Travis…. I told you there was no where you could hide from me. I will get what is rightfully mine! I'll be back… and this time…. I won't be alone."

Made in the USA
Las Vegas, NV
02 December 2021